W9-BKK-246

A Billion-Dollar Family

A bond worth billions!

After graduating Harvard as best mates, Trace Jackson, Wyatt White and Cade Smith formed the billion-dollar company that made them all superrich. Now life has forced them to go in different directions, but they're still as close as can be.

But while they were successful in business, these tycoons haven't been successful in love...until now. Because they're about to meet the women who will change their lives, and their ideas about family, forever!

Trace heads to Tuscany with the aim of forgetting his past and finds so much more in:

Tuscan Summer with the Billionaire

Stranded in paradise with his ex, Cade must reckon with the secrets that broke them apart in:

The Billionaire's Island Reunion

Available now!

Dear Reader,

When I wrote the first book in this series, *Tuscan Summer with the Billionaire*, Cade Smith was always fishing. It was one of those things that surprised me because the guy simply would not fit the mold that I wanted him in. He would march to his own drum.

But that turned out to be cool because it gave me the chance to set an entire book on a private island where anything Reese Farrell wanted could be hers... Even Cade, if she could be brave enough to tell him the real reason she'd broken up with him when they were teenagers.

She has secrets, and she doesn't believe it's possible for her and Cade to have a happily-ever-after. But is it so wrong to want a week? One week in the gorgeous, warm Florida Keys. One week with a guy who makes her swoon. One week to hold in her heart when she returns to her real life in Ohio.

Her secrets forced her to make her peace with being alone. She just wants this one week...

Come with us to the Florida Keys. Bathed in sun, cradled by the sea, the place calls to something in everyone's soul.

Susan Meier

The Billionaire's Island Reunion

—

Susan Meier

PAPL
DISCARDED

If you purchased this book without a cover you should be aware that this book is stolen property. It was reported as "unsold and destroyed" to the publisher, and neither the author nor the publisher has received any payment for this "stripped book."

Recycling programs for this product may not exist in your area.

ISBN-13: 978-1-335-40684-2

The Billionaire's Island Reunion

Copyright © 2021 by Linda Susan Meier

All rights reserved. No part of this book may be used or reproduced in any manner whatsoever without written permission except in the case of brief quotations embodied in critical articles and reviews.

This is a work of fiction. Names, characters, places and incidents are either the product of the author's imagination or are used fictitiously. Any resemblance to actual persons, living or dead, businesses, companies, events or locales is entirely coincidental.

This edition published by arrangement with Harlequin Books S.A.

For questions and comments about the quality of this book, please contact us at CustomerService@Harlequin.com.

Harlequin Enterprises ULC
22 Adelaide St. West, 40th Floor
Toronto, Ontario M5H 4E3, Canada
www.Harlequin.com

Printed in U.S.A.

Susan Meier is the author of over fifty books for Harlequin. *The Tycoon's Secret Daughter* was a Romance Writers of America RITA® Award finalist, and *Nanny for the Millionaire's Twins* won the Book Buyers' Best Award and was a finalist in the National Readers' Choice Awards. Susan is married and has three children. One of eleven children herself, she loves to write about the complexity of families and totally believes in the power of love.

Books by Susan Meier

Harlequin Romance

A Billion-Dollar Family

Tuscan Summer with the Billionaire

Christmas at the Harrington Park Hotel

Stolen Kiss with Her Billionaire Boss

The Missing Manhattan Heirs

Cinderella's Billion-Dollar Christmas
The Bodyguard and the Heiress
Hired by the Unexpected Billionaire

Manhattan Babies

Falling for the Pregnant Heiress

Visit the Author Profile page
at Harlequin.com for more titles.

To my Facebook friends who let me be silly and
funny every morning.

**Praise for
Susan Meier**

"The perfect choice. I read this in one sitting; once
I started, I couldn't put it down. *The Bodyguard
and the Heiress* will put a smile in your heart. What
I love most about Susan Meier's books is the
joy your heart feels as you take the journey with
characters that come to life. Love this book."

—*Goodreads*

CHAPTER ONE

THE HOUSE, A five-bedroom Colonial in Oilville, Ohio, with six bathrooms and an elaborate backyard made for entertaining, was a symbol of everything wrong with Cade Smith's childhood. His parents had made him a pawn in their protracted divorce as they battled over a bunch of two-by-fours and furniture. Neither had really wanted the old-fashioned monstrosity. They just hadn't wanted the other to have it.

At eighteen, he'd prayed for a Solomon-like judge who would cut it in two and ruin it for both of them, then realized they'd already done that to him. With the way they'd ranted about each other to him and torn him up over the choice of who to spend every holiday with, they'd split his life right down the middle, making him live in two different worlds.

He shoved open the door of his rented SUV, stepping out in the chilly April morning air, shaking his head, as he strode to the front entry. He was over all that. Thirty years old and a billionaire with his partners, Trace Jackson and Wyatt White, he'd gotten beyond his mom throwing dishes and his dad buying a gun. He was even over the heartbreak he was sure they caused him with his first love.

He snorted. Did anybody really want to be dating the kid whose parents fought on Main Street, made the preacher cry and put hidden cameras in each other's bedrooms looking for dirt they could use in court?

Reese Farrell hadn't wanted to. That's for sure. When she'd dumped him, she'd shattered his heart so thoroughly, there were days he didn't think he'd survive.

But he had. And he had a great life in Manhattan. So why was the pain of his past roaring through him like the winds of a category five hurricane?

He paused at the door to draw a long, life-sustaining breath, deciding that returning to his small town after twelve years away had to be bringing back all these memories. He hadn't even *thought about* Reese in at least ten of those years. His dad and the gun? As long as Martin Smith still owned it, that was something Cade would have to monitor. No forgetting that.

He pushed open the door of the Colonial.

Blaring hip-hop music greeted him, along with a totally remodeled downstairs. The open floor plan allowed him to see the whole way into the white kitchen that sat beside a family room decorated with a mishmash of furniture. Very Bohemian. Of course, his dad's most recent ex-wife had been about twenty-two—

He rolled his eyes. He had to stop being snarky. His dad had had a stroke. His current trophy girlfriend had run like a rat deserting a sinking ship. His mother didn't give a damn. As always, Cade had to stand in the gap.

"Dad?"

The music swallowed his call. With a sigh, he headed to the den, where the controls for the sound system used to be. Finding another remodeled space, this one an odd shade of green with beanbag chairs his father would never be able to sit in, he scanned the buttons and ended the music.

He walked to the high-ceilinged foyer again. "Dad?"

Muffled voices came from a closed-off room to the right—where the dining room had been when Cade had moved out to attend Harvard. He started toward it, but the door popped open. A woman wearing black yoga pants and a tank top barreled out. Her red hair had been pulled into a short, bouncy ponytail and her green eyes spit fire.

Recognition poured through him like a bucket of ice water. "Reese?"

She halted as if she'd walked into a brick wall. "Cade?"

His heart stopped, along with his breathing. Surely to God she wasn't dating his dad!

She pushed past him. "Did you turn off my music?"

He pivoted to the right, his gaze following her as she marched to the den. Taller now, with full breasts and a perfect butt, she found the controls and in seconds the house filled with hip-hop again.

She stormed out, breezing by him on the way back to the former dining room.

His stomach couldn't take it anymore. He had to ask. "What are you doing here? Are you dating *my dad*?"

Her eyes widened as her mouth fell open. "No! I am not dating your dad! I'm his nurse. His physical therapist gets here in ten minutes. He has to be stretched by then."

The picture that formed in Cade's brain almost made him gag. "You're stretching him?"

"Most of last week I also helped him into the shower. Wanna yell about that too?"

"I wouldn't have to yell, if the music wasn't so loud."

"It's his motivation. Like torture. I don't turn it off until he's done the work."

Relief and humor hit at the same time. He snickered, then chuckled, then out and out belly laughed. "Now, that's worth four plane rides and a forty-minute drive from the airport."

"Yeah. I can see you really raced to get here. He had his stroke over a week ago."

"The doctors said he was fine."

"Your concern is touching."

He could have told her that there'd been an accident in one of his company's warehouses and he'd been in Idaho, answering to OSHA. It wasn't possible to get away, especially not when one of their employees had died. Plus, his dad's doctor had told him the stroke had been minor. Now that the plant manager would be taking over the rest of the details in Idaho, he'd been able to leave. But he didn't feel like sharing that information with a woman he no longer knew. Even if it would exonerate him of not rushing home, it was none of her business. From the day she dumped him like a hot potato, like someone who didn't deserve an explanation, everything in his life became none of her business.

His dad stepped out of the former dining

room, which was now God only knew what if it had been set up so he could stretch and do therapy.

"Cade."

The hushed reverence in his dad's voice almost made Cade feel bad. Almost. His gun-toting, rabble-rousing father had been cleared by his doctors and he looked fine. Sure, his head was bald, and the tank top he wore over sweatpants displayed a pot belly. But, as the doctors had said, the stroke was minor. Two days in the hospital proved there were no signs of aftereffects. He appeared good enough that he shouldn't need a nurse. Though, perhaps whoever ordered the nurse recognized his dad needed a keeper.

Shouting to be heard over the music, his dad said, "Come on! Give your old man a hug."

He stepped forward as his dad did. What began as an awkward squeeze filled with emotion. Damn it. He did love the old coot. If he hadn't been in Idaho dealing with an accident and grieving coworkers, he'd have been here the day the doctors called him, no matter how minor they'd said the stroke had been. His parents might be nuts, but he loved them. Which was the real paradox of being a child. Parents could be bat-smack crazy, and you'd still care for them, protect them, love them.

Unfortunately, his particular parents couldn't be in the same room without fighting. Which was why he never came home—and why he hadn't thought about Reese in over a decade. He'd been more than occupied at Harvard. Then the risky partnership with Wyatt and Trace, that made all three of them billionaires, had taken every ounce of his concentration. Now, the new business needed all their energy.

Cade and his father pulled apart. His dad wiped away tears. Cade blinked his back. He was so relieved to see with his own eyes that his dad was fine that he could barely squelch the emotion.

"You still have five reps of the last stretch to do."

He peered at Reese, strange feelings rumbling through him. He didn't remember her as being so bossy. She'd been happy, the highlight of his senior year in high school.

Funny how he'd never thought of her. He tilted his head. *That wasn't entirely true.*

He'd thought of her on his wedding day, right before he'd stepped out to the altar where the preacher stood. And the thought had been only a weird, fleeting *something*. Not a fully formed memory or wish. More like his dating past flashing before his eyes.

His dad made one final pass over his cheeks

to dry them before he looked at Reese. "Aw, come on! My boy is here."

Reese caught his arm and led him toward the open door. "I don't care. You might be okay with getting yelled at by Yolanda, but she scares me. Get back on the mat."

Cade leaned in and saw the room that had once hosted his birthday dinners was now a home gym.

As his father lowered himself to the mat, Cade said, "You two finish up. I'll go make myself a cup of coffee."

Reese grabbed his father's leg and stretched it over his shoulder. "Whatever."

Cade closed the door and ambled to the kitchen. The weirdness of seeing his first love shuffled through him. If he closed his eyes, he could picture her at sixteen, feel the tingles that always whooshed through him when she was around.

He groaned. Juxtaposed against his worry over his dad's stroke and the emotions rolling through him over losing an employee, thinking about how attracted he'd been to Reese was just plain wrong. He had bigger things to focus on, ponder, examine. A twelve-year-old breakup shouldn't be popping up on his radar. Even if the woman who had broken up with him was in his space for the first time since the quick conversation where she'd given him back his locket.

His brain filled with confusion, as his heart filled with pain. He'd been so stunned and hadn't really understood it was over until she'd refused to take his calls—

Oh, for heaven's sake!

Rehashing all that was foolish on so many levels that he took his coffee outside to the huge stone patio, pulled out his phone and called Wyatt to see how things were going in Idaho.

Reese Farrell relaxed her hold on Martin Smith's foot and slowly lowered his leg to the mat before she lifted it again for the second of five stretches that she would do on each leg. Though the work was easy, it required concentration, which prevented her from thinking about Cade. How good he looked as an adult with his pretty yellow hair and piercing blue eyes. How his golf shirt displayed the muscles of his shoulders and chest and showed absolutely no sign of fat around his middle.

Cade's dad grunted. "You know, it's hard for me to breathe when you press my leg over my shoulder like that."

She shoved the picture of Cade out of her head. After five days of coming to Martin's house every morning, cooking him a healthy breakfast and helping him with his exercises, they'd created a rapport that allowed him to be grouchy and her to be sassy about it because they genuinely liked each other. Five years ago, he'd been the investment counselor who'd advised her on the kind of loan to get to start her business. They'd talked on the phone once a week for about a year, until her company had hit the point where it supported itself. So when he needed a home nurse, he'd called her. Rather than send an employee, she'd kept the job herself. They were friends. Friends who teased each other, but still friends.

"*You* know, if you'd lose that lump of stomach, stretching wouldn't be a problem."

"Nurses and trainers. You're all alike. Always know what's best for everybody while your own life is in shambles."

She gaped at him. "My life is not in shambles. I run a successful home nursing agency."

"Yeah. Yeah. Whatever. You've got some cash. Don't we all?"

"No, Scrooge McDuck. Most people don't have a lot of cash. Myself included. You're the one who taught me to reinvest most of my profits back into the business until I hit the level of income I want."

"Is that why you wouldn't take ten minutes to talk with my son?"

She stole a quick breath to mask the shiver that rolled through her. She hadn't seen Cade in so long there were times she could almost forget he was part of her life. Which had actually been for the best. The night she'd needed him the most, he was at Harvard. Not answering her calls. Probably at a frat party.

The emptiness of how alone she'd been that night still stung. It had taken him four days to call her back. *Four days.* An eternity to a teenager who'd been raped and needed to talk to the man who supposedly loved her.

By the time he finally did return her call, she'd been tongue-tied and confused. She genuinely didn't know how to tell him that someone they knew had violated her in the worst possible way. She'd said nothing and he didn't press, as if he couldn't hear the pain in her voice and didn't realize something terrible had happened to her. The few calls they had after that were filled with talk of his studies, his new friends and, of course, his crazy parents.

When he returned for Thanksgiving vacation, she'd given back his locket—a better symbol of their love, he'd said, than a ring—and he hadn't argued. He'd shoved the necklace in his jeans pocket, walked away and simply never came home again. Not because of her, she was sure. Because of his gun-toting dad and crazy-like-a-fox mother.

And she'd been alone—facing therapy sessions that did help her recover—but still alone. When he'd promised—*promised*—he'd never leave her. He'd said that even away at school, he'd find a way to keep them close.

And the one time she really needed him, he hadn't answered his phone.

Was it any wonder she'd put all that in a box of memories and never opened it?

"When we're done, you're having coffee with him."

"I have other clients to get to."

"No, you don't. You told me that every Friday at noon, you're off the clock because I'm your last client."

She gritted her teeth, ignoring him.

"Come on," he cajoled, then grunted again when she stretched his leg over his shoulder. "One cup of coffee can't hurt."

She said nothing.

"I always felt bad that you and Cade broke up." He winced. "I might have been oblivious in the past, but even a small stroke makes a guy think. You dumped him because he never came home from university when my ex and

I were throwing barbs at each other across Main Street."

"And sometimes plates." That wasn't how their breakup had happened, but there was no need to correct Martin. He didn't know the truth. Some fast action on her parents' part and the county district attorney had kept the situation quiet. Plus, Finn McCully wasn't sixteen. The court records had been sealed. Martin had no idea—no one in town had any idea—that Finn and his parents hadn't moved away for a new job. They'd relocated so they could hide that Finn was in a juvenile detention center.

Martin laughed. "Yeah, we were nuts through that divorce."

She gaped at him. "You cannot believe your behavior was funny."

He sobered. "Everything is funny once a few years have gone by."

Her stomach turned and she eased his leg to the floor, finishing the last of his stretches. Unwanted memories flitted through her brain—

Refusing alcohol from Finn, after he'd lured her under the bleachers at a Friday night football game.

The horrible realization that she was being followed as she walked home alone when her friend Janie veered off onto the driveway for her house.

The anger in Finn McCully's voice—"You think you're so special..."

She closed her eyes, pulled in a deep breath and dispelled the rest of the memory as it tried to form. She never let herself think about that night. She relegated it to a box as her therapist had told her and locked it tight, so it couldn't hurt her anymore—

But the image of the box, though powerful, worked only to a point. The trauma and damage of being raped rippled through her life, manifesting as a cautious streak so strong and so tight her rules for dating and sometimes simply living were ingrained to the point she didn't even have to think about them anymore. They subconsciously guided her life, her choices.

No one would ever hurt her again.

She took a breath, forced herself back to the present and Martin Smith. "Not everything becomes funny after a few years."

"Sure, it does!" Martin insisted as he did his three-part maneuver to get his roly-poly self off the floor: get on all fours, hoist butt into the air, pull torso upright.

He let out a "Whew," then said, "Cade never visiting probably *was* painful. But he was a kid trying to get control of his life. He couldn't do that here with me and his mom making a circus of our divorce. Plus, over a decade has gone by. I think you two need a fresh start."

"I don't."

Finn would have never come within ten feet of her had Cade been home to go with her to the football game. Even if Cade hadn't been home, if he'd returned her call that night, she could have opened up to him, sought his support about her rape. But no. He wasn't around Friday night or Saturday or Sunday. Her calls to him all went to voice mail.

When he finally returned her call, she'd frozen. Lost her nerve. Couldn't tell him any of it—

Damn it!

She'd worked with a therapist to forget all this and one five-minute encounter with Cade in Martin's foyer had it tumbling through her like an avalanche.

To get that memory out of her brain, she picked up the mat and rolled it, then remembered Martin's physical therapist would need it and spread it out on the floor again.

Luckily, the doorbell rang. "And there's Yolanda now."

Martin huffed out a sigh. "Send her in." He grinned. "Then go get that cup of coffee with Cade."

She left without answering and walked

to the foyer, where she opened the door for Yolanda. They shared a few pleasantries, then she grabbed her jacket and sneaked out without a goodbye to Martin or another word to Cade.

They had nothing to say to each other and all he did was remind her of the worst night of her life. So, no. She wouldn't have coffee with him. If that meant not saying goodbye to Martin, so be it.

CHAPTER TWO

THAT AFTERNOON, when Reese's phone rang and Martin's picture popped up on the screen, she regretted not staying long enough to say goodbye to him. She knew his heart was in the right place. Though his stroke had been minor, it scared him enough that he'd had a major change of personality. He'd told her that being reminded you won't live forever gives a person perspective, and for the past week he'd constantly looked for ways to be a nicer, more compassionate guy.

Despite their sarcastic banter, she'd been encouraging that. She couldn't ignore him now or he might lose the progress he'd made.

Sitting back on the desk chair of her cluttered home office, she punched the icon to answer her phone. "Okay. I'm sorry for not saying goodbye."

"No biggie. Actually, *I* want to apologize."

Her eyebrows rose. "Really?"

"Yeah. Yeah. You and I have been over this. I'm a changed man. I'm starting to see other people's needs. You didn't want to hear what I had to say this morning about you and Cade. And that's your right. I shouldn't have pushed. Which is why I'm going to add a gift to my apology."

Pleased that he really was changing, she smiled. "No need for that."

"I insist. I have a beach house in the Florida Keys. It's yours for as long as you want."

She blinked. "What?"

"A beach house. In the Keys. Yours for as long as you can take off work. I made your flight arrangements. I'll text you the ticket number so you can print the boarding passes. Return flight is open. You can stay a week. You can stay ten days. Hell, you can stay a month if you want."

Her breath caught. "Is this for real?"

"Yes."

She bit her lower lip. Not only did she have a business to run, but accepting his offer felt like taking advantage of a client. "I couldn't."

He laughed. "Why not? We've been in each other's lives and each other's business for five years. I'm not just a client. You were *my* client. And now we're *friends*." He sighed. "Come on, kid. We both know how much you did for me since the stroke, when there was no one else around to help me. But I'm good now. I've got a housekeeper for company during the day and Yolanda has agreed to do my stretches before my therapy." His voice softened. "The damned beach house sits empty most of the time. Look at it as a friend lending you his beach house."

When he put it that way, his offer made sense. She thought about her schedule and realized she had enough employees to cover her work. And after seeing Cade, awful memories of Finn's foul breath and fear kept clawing at her. A few days away might be just what she needed. Not only to clear her head but also to ensure she wouldn't accidentally run into Cade while he visited his dad.

"You're sure?"

"Yes. You're a good person. The kind of person I want to be someday. So consider the trip my thanks for showing me the way."

"I'll have to move some patients…"

"You have enough staff to handle it," he said as if he'd read her mind a few minutes before. "Just go. Take the break. The house is on the beach, stocked with food. All you need is to get yourself to the airport. Your flight is tomorrow morning at eight. I've even arranged for someone to pick you up and get you to the house."

The thought of going to a tropical paradise

filled her with a joy she couldn't remember ever feeling. Not just a way to snuff out those damned memories, but some time to herself. No work. No clients. Just sun and sand. She hadn't had a vacation in five years—

"You know what? I will take a week at your beach house. Thank you."

Martin said, "My pleasure," then hung up the phone.

She called her assistant and instructed her to check the schedule to see if her clients really could be covered, then raced upstairs, lugged her suitcase from under the bed and began filling it. Realizing it might be nice to have company, she called two friends, neither of whom could join her on such short notice, but she didn't care. Once her assistant told her that her personal clients had easily been reassigned, nothing but happiness filled her brain.

Seven days to herself would be the best gift any friend had ever given her.

When Cade entered his dad's brand-new silver, gray and white kitchen the next morning, an attractive middle-aged woman dressed in scrubs stood by the counter making coffee.

"Good morning."

She glanced over. "Good morning. You must be Martin's son. I'm only here to make sure your dad takes his morning pills. Then he's on his own."

He walked to the refrigerator, found bagels and headed for the toaster. "Are you sure that's a good idea?"

"Yeah. Your dad's fine. His doctor's being cautious, though, having home nurses regulate his meds for the first few weeks and Yolanda coming in to get him on the right path with physical activity. I think his doctor's using the physical therapy as a gateway into a regular exercise habit as part of a cardiac rehabilitation program."

The words weren't fully out of her mouth before his dad walked in. This morning, he looked more like his fifty-six years than he had the day before. He had color in his cheeks and wore jeans and a T-shirt, not scruffy workout clothes.

He pointed at the bagels. "Don't make yourself breakfast. I have a housekeeper for that."

Cade stopped. "You do?"

"Yeah. She'll be here in ten minutes to make breakfast and tidy the house."

The pretty nurse winked at Cade. "And to make sure he eats right. Not just deli meat and slabs of cheese on white bread."

The nurse took a few pills from bottles that she'd pulled from the cabinet on the far right and handed them to his dad with a glass of water.

He threw them into his mouth, chugged the water and set the glass down with a satisfied clunk. "Happy now?"

The nurse laughed. "Yes."

Cade tilted his head, for the first time realizing his dad's nurse wasn't Reese. Emotion-filled memories spiraled through him. Things he'd forgotten suddenly poured through his brain. Reese had been the center of his world. He'd dated before he met her—mostly taking girls to movies or football games—but there had been something about Reese, a click, that had nearly rendered him speechless. One day after study hall, he'd walked her to her next class, and that night they'd talked on the phone for hours. The following Saturday night they'd had their first date. They'd been inseparable for the year after that.

Then his parents had decided to divorce, the war over the Colonial had begun and he'd happily left for Harvard. But without warning, she'd become weird with him when he called. Then she'd stopped answering his calls. So, he'd come home for Thanksgiving and instead of the happy surprise he'd been expecting, she'd broken up with him with very little explanation. She just gave him back his locket and told him they were through.

The pain of that rose as if it were yesterday—

He shook his head to end it. He thought he'd stopped these silly memories the day before.

"So, you had your pills." The nurse's voice interrupted Cade's thoughts. "And your housekeeper is pulling into the driveway. That means I'm off."

"Off your rocker," Cade's dad replied, then ruined the joke by hugging the nurse. "Go. See you tomorrow. Same time."

Cade stared at his dad, as the nurse collected her purse and walked out the back door.

"She's a good girl."

His eyes narrowed. "You're not thinking about dating her, are you?"

"For a guy who has no one in his own life, you worry a lot about my dates."

"I'm home for a week or so, then I'm going to my beach house. I don't want to be blindsided."

"Then don't visit your mother. She's dating the preacher. Got religion, but I don't think it's going to last. If you had visited a week from now, you could have probably avoided that phase altogether."

He laughed.

His dad got a cup of the coffee the nurse had

made and walked to the table. "This is decaf, you know."

Cade groaned.

"Sorry. Doctor's orders. At least until he's sure my blood pressure is under control." He sat and motioned to the pot. "Really, it's not so bad. Reese found this expensive stuff that's actually pretty good."

The mention of her name brought back memories again. Unexpectedly happy ones. First walk in the moonlight. First kiss.

His chest tightened at the same time that his brain tried to wrap his head around what was happening. He hadn't seen Reese in twelve years. He shouldn't care about a high school fling. Yet something about the way she'd broken up with him seemed off—

"It was weird that you had to run into her yesterday," his dad said as he added cream to his coffee. "Had I known you were coming I could have scheduled things differently. In fact, if you're staying for a week, maybe you could be out of the house while she's here."

He caught Cade's gaze and Cade's eyes narrowed. His dad had *that* look on his face. The one he got when he was lying. But how could asking him to leave the house be lying?

It couldn't. Once again, he was misreading things, making too much of things because his brain was on overwhelm from the accident at the warehouse. His mind was crammed with facts and figures and sorrow. Not to mention a sense of responsibility that just wouldn't quit.

"I gave her today off since you're here. But she's the nurse I want monitoring my meds. Though I don't really need her to stay full days, she usually insists. Wicked Yahtzee player. But I beat her in Uno," his dad said, talking about two games they'd always played when he was a kid.

More memories drifted through him. The bad ones this time. How crushed he was that Reese had dumped him, but worse that she'd never satisfactorily explained why.

His nerve endings buzzed with indignation. Confusing thoughts rolled through his head about fate and responsibility and the simple, horrible truth of how much of life was out of a person's hands.

He stopped the thoughts, took a breath and told his brain to slow down. But he knew it wouldn't. Not because of a twelve-year-old breakup, but because he wasn't as nonchalant about the accident at the warehouse as he wanted everyone to believe. It was his job to make sure all companies followed OSHA regulations. His job to determine risk.

He took another breath. Though the logical part of his brain accepted that he had done everything he was supposed to do—so had the warehouse's general manager—and accidents happened, something inside him simply couldn't settle down.

Dealing with his dad and seeing Reese was just too much when added to the confusion and guilt he had over someone in one of their operations losing his life.

Dying. Someone had died on his watch.

He couldn't think about it without his chest hollowing out and his breathing going shallow.

"Of course, you could always fly to Manhattan and return in a few weeks, after the doctor clears me from needing a nurse to check my meds every day." His dad laughed. "Hey, by then, your mom will be over the preacher and you'll be able to visit her too."

"I only have the next two weeks off. Trace and Wyatt are running the business without me so they can each get time off around the holidays."

"Always hated that you stopped coming home for the holidays." Martin took a long drink of coffee. "Sure, you shuttle your mom and me to Manhattan for bits of your free time, but those visits are short too because you're always prepping to hop on a plane for that island of yours." He glanced at Cade. "How is that island?"

"Warm and sunny," Cade said wistfully. That was what he really needed. A week in the sun to sort things out.

"Okay. So, go there. Then pop in here on your way back to Manhattan so you can visit your mother."

"Since when do you care if I visit my mother?"

"Since I had a stroke and realized life is too short to be a horrible person." He motioned toward the door with his hands. "Shoo. I'm fine. I'll be here when you get back from your fishing paradise."

"I don't know…"

His dad sighed. "Cade, do I have to spell this out for you? That nurse that just left? She's cute. She's smart. She's unlike anybody I've ever dated. And I have a shot with her. I know it."

Cade frowned. Now, he understood his father's weird babbling. He wasn't lying. He was manipulating, trying to figure out a way to get rid of Cade so he could have alone time with the nurse.

Which wasn't such a bad thing. Not only was the nurse intelligent and pretty; she was also closer to his dad's age.

"Come on. You're harshing my buzz."

"If you mean that I'm in the way, harshing my buzz is not the phrase to use."

"Who cares? Get lost. Come back when your mother will be available. I know she misses you."

Leaning against the coffee counter, Cade considered that. He liked the new man his father was becoming. Especially dating a woman who really could be a partner for him. Plus, a trip to the island sounded good. He didn't want to see Reese anymore and relive a heartbreak he'd gotten over a decade ago. Especially not when he was dealing with the death of someone for whom he was responsible. He might not have been Roger's direct boss, but he owned the company that employed him. He had feelings rolling around in him that he didn't understand. He needed some time, and he was smart enough to know that.

His dad was fine, and his mother would be visitable in a week. It made more sense to go to the island now and spend time here later.

He pushed away from the counter. "You know what? I think I will have a cup of the decaf. Then head out for the island."

His dad smiled stupidly.

But why not? Nothing about his dad was normal. And memories of Reese wouldn't let him alone. Which—after twelve years—was just plain odd.

He needed to get away. What better place than his own island?

CHAPTER THREE

CADE CAST DENNIS AUDREY a weird look, as his pilot took the helicopter into the air to fly him from West Keys Airport to his island. Dennis wasn't one for small talk, but he also wasn't the kind of guy to grin without reason. Yet, his pilot grinned as he glided the helicopter into the sky.

Suddenly, the sound of Dennis's voice filled his earphones. "Storm." Dennis pointed as he said the one word.

Cade followed the direction of his finger and saw thunderheads forming.

Dennis's voice filled his earphones again. "You won't be coming back tonight."

Cade frowned. "I don't want to come back tonight."

"Good, because the approaching storm is going to be a doozy."

He knew about storms in this part of the world. They could be vicious. He hadn't checked the weather, but before taking off his pilot obviously had.

Still, it was unusual that Dennis made a point to tell him he wouldn't be coming back that night.

They touched down on the helipad on the far edge of the island, where a space to take off and land had been carved into the dense foliage. Dennis unloaded Cade's duffel from the helicopter, but Cade waved him off when he wanted to carry it to one of the bikes stored in the small shed to the right.

"I can carry one little duffel bag twenty feet. I'll call you when I'm ready to leave."

Dennis grinned again. "Sure thing." He saluted and climbed into the helicopter again.

It took off as Cade tossed his duffel to the basket behind the seat of his bike and slid on.

He closed his eyes and drew a breath, then another, then another, letting his body relax. This was why he'd bought this island. The peace and quiet that surrounded him was all his. He was far enough away from other landowners that he didn't get their ambient noise, but close enough that he could party with his neighbors if he wanted to.

Right now, a little peace and quiet sounded like just what he needed.

Pedaling the bike on the wide path to his retreat, he smiled as his muscles loosened. The big yellow house came into view. It was perfect for hosting a New Year's Eve week or weekend and yet not so enormous that he couldn't stay there by himself.

Climbing the few steps to the front door, he pulled in another long drink of tropical air and looked around. When he was a kid, he'd told himself that someday he'd have a place far, far away to go to when his parents made him a laughingstock. And though his parents' arguments didn't matter anymore, it was still fun that he'd achieved that goal.

He punched in the code for the front door, walked inside and frowned at the breeze blowing in from the ocean. He knew a storm was on the way, but it shouldn't be blowing inside his house—

Unless the back door was open?

He walked through the high-ceilinged foyer with the sunburst chandelier, passing the mostly white kitchen with bright orange designer floor tiles, and saw the back door had been folded to the left so that the living room and patio formed one big space.

Checking to be sure no one was in the infinity pool or the outdoor kitchen with a stone pizza oven and state-of-the-art grill, he dropped his duffel and raced to the door intending to close it. But he saw a woman sprawled facedown on a chaise lounge in the patio area. Lying on her tummy, she let one arm fall to her right and had her face buried in the soft cushion beneath her.

He'd heard of people paying housekeepers or groundskeepers to get the codes for houses that were empty more than they were used, but he'd never actually found an uninvited guest in his house—

On his own private island—where there were no police.

No one to call to get rid of her.

He stepped out onto the patio, then stealthily made his way over to the interloper. Temptation was strong to haul her cute little butt in the pink polka-dot bikini off the chaise. But he wasn't like that. Sure, he would investigate who let her in and fire that person, but he'd do it sensibly.

He reached down to shake her awake, but when he saw her top was unhooked so she wouldn't get a tan line on her back, touching her didn't feel right either.

He snatched his hand away.

"Get up," he said in his sternest *I'm a billionaire* voice.

She didn't stir.

"Get up!" he said, louder and angrier than the first time.

When she still didn't move, he yelled, "What the hell are you doing in my house?"

Finally awake, she lifted her head, groggily turned it to the left and probably saw his denim-covered legs. She bounced from her stomach into a seated position in what seemed like one fluid movement.

Grasping her top in place over her breasts, she said, "Cade?"

Trying to keep his eyes on her face and away from any exposed flesh, he said, "Reese?"

She fumbled to reattach her bikini top and he pivoted away to give her privacy. But it was too late. His brain had taken a mental picture of her pale skin, full breasts and belly button ring. He was pretty sure the shiny red part was her birthstone.

"You can turn around now."

As he did, she grabbed a pink floral cover-up and shimmied into it. "What are you doing here?"

He gaped at her. "What are you doing here? This is my island!"

"No. It's your dad's beach house."

"My dad doesn't own a beach house. He uses *my island.*"

A few seconds passed as that seemed to settle into her brain. "You own a whole island?"

Sun shimmered off her red hair that had dried in ringlets, probably after a dip in the pool or the ocean. Her green eyes held his gaze. And all he could think about was the summer they'd spent at the pool in the backyard of the Colonial, while both his parents were at work. Sometimes he'd invite friends to join them. Other times he didn't. Lots of times he just wanted her to himself.

He'd been so crazy in love with her. Not merely because she brought sanity to his otherwise chaotic life, but because she was fun to be around. A kid with a normal childhood, she knew how to make lemonade and no-bake chocolate oatmeal cookies from ingredients she found around the house. But she also loved playing video games on his advanced gaming system and lounging at the pool. Always dressed in a tiny bikini, she'd about driven his seventeen-year-old self crazy with lust.

When they'd finally given in to their feelings, their romance had gone from fun and exuberant to passionate and important. He'd have done anything for her.

The memory filled his chest with longing for simpler times, simpler needs. He got rid of it with a deep breath that puffed his lungs before he blew it out, releasing the yearning for something that could never be. Something that might not have ever actually existed, if the way she'd broken up with him was anything to go by.

"Yes. I own an entire island." He waited a beat. "What are you doing here?"

"Your dad told me I could use *his* beach house." She snorted. "He told me he was changing, getting generous."

"Yeah. Generous with my house." Cade ran his hand along the back of his neck. "He kind of persuaded me to spend the next week here… something about my mom dating the preacher."

An unexpected, joyful laugh poured from her. "Yeah. That's a real hoot. They're like the odd couple. Been together almost a month."

"Dad doesn't think it will last more than another week."

"There's a betting pool at the diner. I took three more weeks."

"You're gonna lose your money."

She grinned. "Only if your dad is right."

He chuckled, then drew in another breath. It might be odd to talk normally with her after twelve years of not seeing each other. But somehow they'd tumbled from awkward to normal in about three seconds. It felt good. *He* felt good. Almost himself.

"Looks like he set us up."

She straightened her cover-up. "Yeah. He

wanted me to talk to you yesterday, but I needed to get on with my work."

He saw it then. A wisp of something that came to her green eyes. It could have been sorrow or sadness, but when he gave it a few seconds of thought, he decided it looked more like exhaustion. She banked it quickly, as if she were accustomed to doing that, and something warm and protective filled him. Probably from the memories of how he'd felt about her all those years ago, how he would have done anything for her.

The weirdness of the situation returned. He combed his fingers through his short hair. "This is odd."

She tightened her hold on the cover-up. "Tell me about it."

"One of us should leave—"

"I will."

He didn't want to go, but her leaving didn't feel right. He sighed. "Not tonight." As if on cue, thunder rumbled. "Storm."

Her chin lifted. "Then I'll leave in the morning."

She said it as if she were angry at him, as if she had a reason to be angry with him, and that attitude went through him like a knife. That was how she'd been the day she broke up with him. Distant. Angry. As if he'd done something god awful. And he hadn't. He'd been too busy with the start of the school year at an Ivy League university. He might have been the smartest kid at his high school, but at Harvard he was average. If she hadn't been able to respect or understand how difficult his first year had been, then she wasn't the girl he'd thought.

He turned to walk into the house. "Sure. Leave in the morning. That's fine."

He wanted the memories of his past to stop, so he could clear his head. Her leaving was the way to assure that. If she was still angry about something he didn't even know he'd done, she could leave.

No problem.

With rain pounding on the roof, sounding like kettledrums, Reese went to the room where she'd stowed her luggage and toiletries case.

It wasn't so much a "room" as a suite with a sitting room in front, a huge yellow, tan and black bedroom with a king-size bed and a private bath that looked like a spa.

Staring at the two-person black-tiled shower with rain heads and total-body massaging jets, beside a freestanding black tub on black and white octagonal tiles, she suddenly gasped.

What if she'd taken the master bedroom?

Wouldn't it be embarrassing to have Cade

mindlessly climb the steps that night and crawl into bed with her?

Her heart didn't know whether to swoon or beat out of her chest. She didn't date much. Rarely slept with anyone. Therapy had gotten her beyond her fear of sex. It was a normal, healthy sign of affection and when she found someone she genuinely cared for, she could be all in.

But she was particular, and technically she didn't know Cade anymore. Even though he'd become an absolutely gorgeous man, the whoosh of desire that washed through her was foreign.

And wrong.

He'd deserted her when she'd needed him most. He'd proved himself to be untrustworthy—

Still—

A private island, a luscious man—

Stop.

No one was crawling into bed with anyone. It was against Rule Number Two. *Must know your partner.* She hadn't seen Cade in so long that he was a stranger now.

It would also be against Rule Number Three. *No one-night stands.*

She shook her head. She hadn't had to refer to her rules in a long time. After over a decade, most of them, like Rule Number One, *Never put yourself in a sketchy situation*, were ingrained behaviors. The fact that she was remembering the rules her sixteen-year-old self had created in therapy told her something was "off" here. The thought that risky behavior even tiptoed into her brain floored her. Cade might be a stranger, but deep down she knew he was a nice guy.

Wasn't he?

He seemed to be.

But she also couldn't drop her rules without as much as an eye bat. She had to ascertain the best plan of action with him, especially how to behave around him tonight.

The storm made their situation worse. Without the driving rain, one of them could be on the beach, the other in the house. With the rain, there was nowhere to go.

Lightning streaked across the black sky.

Yep. They were stuck inside together. Would they end up eating together? Or watching TV together? Plus, if she'd taken his room, she had to give it back. So, would there be an odd dance in the hall as she carried her repacked bags to another room, and he carried his big duffel into this one?

And if this wasn't his room, where *was* he sleeping?

They had to have a chat. The sooner the better. Then she could watch TV in whatever room she ended up bunking, repack and maybe even be gone before he woke the next morning.

She quickly slid into yoga pants and a pink T-shirt and headed downstairs. She found Cade in the white kitchen with the stunning orange-and-white Moroccan design floor tiles with a complementary orange backsplash. Bread, deli meat, cheese and a jar of mustard were scattered on the big center island. Answering at least one question. Would she have to eat dinner with him?

No. She could make herself a sandwich while he had everything out on the counter and then take it to another room.

Relief smoothed her ruffled nerve endings.

Plus, while she made the sandwich that she would take to her room to eat, she could get answers to her other questions, calm herself and be able to sleep before going home the next morning.

He glanced up and saw her in front of the island. "Sandwich?"

"You read my mind." She got a plate from a cupboard and began layering bread, meat and cheese.

"There's beer in the fridge."

Her hand stopped halfway to the mustard. "Beer?"

"Or soft drinks. There's a wine room behind the den," he said casually as if every house in the world had a wine room. "And an actual bar in the family room in case you like cocktails or whisky on the rocks."

Rule Number Six, *Be careful around alcohol*, popped into her head. She hadn't been drinking but Finn had.

She took a breath. Hating that the most horrible night of her life kept running through her brain, she brought out the mental box again and shoved those thoughts inside. Then she locked it and tossed the key.

"I think I'll just have a soft drink. Is there anything without caffeine?"

He snorted. "What? Did you become a Mormon after we stopped dating?"

Her answer was quick and every bit as sarcastic as his. "Did you become snarky after we stopped dating?"

He rolled his eyes and she pulled back her sarcasm. She had information to get.

"The pilot, Dennis, took my things to the bedroom at the top of the stairs. If that's the master, I'll happily move."

"That's not the master." He put a slice of bread on top of what looked to be a work-of-art sandwich and headed for the fridge. Pulling out a bottle of beer, he said, "Master is on the third floor." He grinned. "Better view. I own it. I get it."

"I heard the rumors that you'd gotten rich."

He shrugged. "I found two partners who love to work. Wyatt is the brains of the operation. The guy with the big ideas. Trace is our memory and fact-checker. He's our detail guy."

"And you?"

"I like to think of myself as daily operations."

The normal conversation went a long way to nudge her rules out of her head as she began remembering what an average guy he was for a kid who'd been so smart. "Daily operations?"

"Trace hires and fires employees, but I handle benefits and salaries. I'm the actuarial science guy. I assess risk. Get insurance when needed or tell Trace and Wyatt to pull back from projects or investments where the risk outweighs the reward."

He took a sudden breath, and an odd expression came to his face as if something he'd said about risk brought him up short.

She almost asked him about it. Instead, labeling her curiosity as inappropriate given that she was leaving, she said, "Still a geek."

"Maybe. But look how it's paid off."

He said it easily, but his face contorted again. Did he really believe it had paid off?

It struck her that he was alone for his vacation. There was no ring on his finger. There were no kids clamoring to come with Daddy to the family's private island. His friends were his partners. Business associates.

He truly might be wondering if it was worth it—
That was none of her business.

Rummaging through the fridge, she found a soft drink without caffeine and picked up her plate with her sandwich. "So, I don't have to change rooms?"

He frowned. "No."

"Okay. Good night, then."

"You're going to bed?"

"No. I'll watch some TV upstairs."

He nodded. "Okay."

"I'll also call Dennis before I settle in and be gone in the morning."

"Don't call now. Wait until an hour before you're ready to go. Give him the night off with his family."

"Okay." She smiled slightly, not wanting to look like an ungrateful guest, but also impressed that he protected his employee's time off. She'd heard most rich guys were selfish. It was good to see he hadn't changed much from the nice boy she'd dated…the first guy she'd made love with.

"I'll call tomorrow."

"Okay."

With a nod, she turned and walked through the foyer to the main steps and up to the room she was using.

Rain pounded the sliding glass door that led to a small balcony with a view of the ocean that had stolen her breath when she arrived.

She sat on the sofa in the sitting room, ate her sandwich and watched an outdated sitcom she found on the TV that had to be connected to a satellite with supergood reception.

Then she changed into her pajamas and climbed into a bed with sheets so soft she sighed with contentment.

She supposed she'd always known Cade would make something of himself. He'd been at the top of their class. Plus, his parents were both hard workers.

And crazy. She couldn't forget that working so hard had made them nuts when it came time to divide their assets.

Thoughts of her year with Cade flitted through her and she relaxed into the pillow to the soothing sound of rain that had finally slowed to a pitter patter. She remembered meeting his parents. Remembered the day she realized just how smart he was. Remembered their first kiss.

In the moonlight.

Her heart had about drummed out of her chest. God, she'd loved him.

First love, she supposed, was the strongest. First real kiss. First time of trusting someone with your heart. First true connection. Which was why their first time of making love had been so special.

She closed her eyes. It had been so, so special. And every time after that had been remarkable. They grew to the point where they could make lovemaking fun, like playing, or intense like giving their hearts all over again.

Which was why it was so hard to believe he'd hadn't taken her calls that weekend. Hadn't been there for her—

In her brain, she found a new box. Opened it. Put in the memory of Cade not taking her calls, leaving her alone to face the aftershocks of being raped. Then mentally locked it and tossed it into the beautiful blue ocean just beyond this house.

She fell asleep forcing herself to think about soft waves and fish.

She didn't want to like him. Not because he was a terrible person, but because when push came to shove, he hadn't been there for her.

But maybe that was lucky.

Besides the rape, there was something else he didn't know about her. If they had stayed together, she would have had to tell him.

And just like her ex, Tony, he probably would have dumped her too.

CHAPTER FOUR

CADE AMBLED INTO the kitchen the next morning and frowned when he glanced through the sliding glass door and saw the mess on the patio. The wind had been sufficient to shake leaves from the trees and even a few branches.

He could call somebody to clean up. He had two groundskeepers under contract. Either would arrive at a moment's notice. But a little physical activity would go a long way to clearing his head.

He opened the fridge and almost drank milk straight from the carton, but remembered Reese was there.

The carton stopped midway to his mouth. *Reese.* He'd thought about her all night. When he finally did fall asleep, he dreamed about her. About happy times. About laughter and intensity. About feelings he hadn't felt before or since.

Not even with Brenda, his ex-wife, which

he supposed should have been a red flag. And might have been why memories of Reese had popped into his head right before he'd walked out to the altar to get married. At the time, he'd given himself some jibber jabber about Reese being his first love. That's why he'd thought of her. But what if his brain had really been trying to tell him what he felt for Reese had been real love and what he felt for Brenda wasn't?

He shook off the notion. Particularly since he did not believe what he and Reese felt had been real love. Otherwise, she wouldn't have unceremoniously ditched him.

After finding a glass, he poured himself some milk, made a bagel and headed outside. He took two bites of the bagel, then set it on the small patio table beside the first chaise lounge. Fresh morning air filled his lungs. The sun warmed the space, promising a hot day. The ocean lay before him like a blue goddess. The whole world was silent.

On a normal visit, once he cleaned the pool, he'd shuck his shorts and skinny-dip. With Reese there he couldn't do that. Though they had. All those summers ago, when they were young and life was easy, they'd made love in the pool. They would lay naked in the sun for hours talking about everything. And then one day it was over. Gone.

It had never added up, if only because Reese was the kind of girl who should have understood his first few weeks at Harvard were an adjustment. He'd told her what he was dealing with. She'd seemed to understand. Yet, when he'd finally come home for Thanksgiving, she hadn't been happy to see him. She'd dumped him.

He'd assumed it was because she'd found somebody else, and that caused so much pain he'd thrown himself into his schoolwork as a way to forget.

And he had.

Especially since he'd never come home again after that.

He returned to his bagel, took another bite and walked to the small cedar cabana to get the skimmer. Eventually everything would be drawn toward the waterfall of the infinity pool and be filtered in the catch, but he wanted to swim *now*. Thinking about Reese might be pushing aside thoughts of Roger Burkey's death but thinking about Reese wasn't good for him either.

So many unanswered questions that seemed to somehow knit into his bad marriage. Otherwise, why would he have remembered Reese before walking to the altar to marry Brenda? If he'd known why Reese had dumped him, would he have been smarter about the woman he'd chosen to marry?

He frowned. That didn't seem right. It didn't really connect or make sense.

But there was no denying his marriage had been a huge mistake. Not only had Brenda been a horrible choice for a partner—who'd made his life miserable with demands and public arguments—but also when they'd divorced, she'd wanted half his share of the corporation he owned with Wyatt and Trace.

Reese hadn't even kept a silly locket. She'd returned the one and only gift he'd given her.

Brenda had been so different from Reese that if he really took this to the logical conclusion, he might think he'd chosen Brenda for just that reason.

After all, Reese had hurt him.

Still, he couldn't shake the feeling that he'd done something wrong that caused her to break up with him. Given that she was the one who'd dumped him, she shouldn't be angry with him right now.

Yet, she clearly was.

The first panel of the sliding glass door opened. It folded into the second, which folded into the third, which folded into the fourth, opening his living space to the patio.

Wincing, Reese walked out. Wearing yoga

pants and a T-shirt, she looked like she'd just woken up.

"Sorry. Every time I try to open only the first panel, the whole thing opens."

Her shy smile sent warmth through him, a longing that wanted to connect the past to the present. To figure all this out.

Which was stupid. Pointless...

Wasn't it?

He angled the skimmer over the pool. "If you only need to open the first panel, you have to be careful not to hit the button on the side of the handle."

"Oh."

He dragged the skimmer through the water, then pulled it out and dumped the leaves, branches and fronds in a small area off to the right, away from the patio. "Where's your breakfast?"

"I usually don't eat breakfast."

"There are coffee pods and a one-cup brewer if you're interested."

"Thanks. I am. I might not eat breakfast but I love my morning coffee." She turned to return to the house, then paused and faced him again. "And I wanted to say I'm sorry."

He froze. He hadn't exactly waited twelve years to hear her say that, but his eighteen-year-old self had been insulted, wounded, *hurt* that she'd discarded him without explanation. Hearing her apologize now wasn't merely surprising; it was unexpectedly welcome.

His chest loosened, but he couldn't quite figure out what to do with her apology. It didn't explain why she'd broken up with him, and something inside him desperately wanted to know what he'd done. And if he'd been the one to do something wrong, why was she apologizing?

"What exactly are you sorry for?"

"I didn't know your dad was setting us up. But I really should have thought this through and realized he probably didn't own a beach house. Somebody in town would have mentioned it. If nothing else, your mother would have griped about it. I should have seen through his offer."

Disappointment rattled through him. Then he called himself an idiot. Just because he'd thought about her and their past the night before didn't mean she had. And twelve years had gone by. He was an older, wiser version of the eighteen-year-old who'd been hurt by her. Why did he keep going over this in his head?

So he wouldn't think about Roger Burkey?

Maybe. But every time he and Reese talked, he got a nudge of a hint that he'd done something to make her dump him. And that really bothered him. He had absolutely no idea what he could have done, except that he was so busy at Harvard that he hadn't even had much time to talk on the phone. Still... She'd seemed to understand that. Or so he'd thought.

Their breakup was the one unsettled thing in his life. Even his bad marriage and subsequent divorce had sorted itself. His relationship with Reese was like a big question mark. And maybe this was fate's way of forcing him to put a period at the end of their sentence. He hadn't seen her in twelve years. Probably wouldn't ever see her again. This might be his one shot at closing that book.

He glanced over at her, saw her draw a long, deep breath as if enjoying the island's morning air, cleaned by last night's storm, as she took in the white sand and ocean before her. Tall and beautiful, with red hair that sparkled in the sun, she looked at his paradise with the kind of yearning that couldn't be hidden. She wanted to stay, and maybe she needed this time away as much as he did.

His curiosity spiked again. He had absolutely no clue what had happened to her in twelve years. As much as he wanted to close the book with her, he also just plain wanted to know how she'd been.

"Have you called Dennis yet?"

"No. I thought I'd have coffee and pack first. That way I would be ready when he got here."

Her logical voice reminded him of the Reese he'd known before she'd split them up, and he said, "Sounds like the Reese I know. Organized. Thorough."

She faced him with a smile and all he saw was *his* Reese. The girl who'd loved life, *loved him*.

"Funny you didn't say that I was happy."

"You were always happy." But the shadows had returned to her green eyes again, and he suddenly didn't want closure as much as he wanted to make things right. Clearly, he'd done something for her to break up with him, and even if she decided not to tell him what it was, maybe doing a good deed for her could appease the weird feelings inside him.

"Don't call."

She faced him, her green eyes confused. "What?"

"Don't call Dennis. Stay."

"I don't want you to have to leave your own house."

"I'm not going. We'll stay here together. The island is almost twenty acres. There's a beach, a pool, a big house…and bigger islands where you might want to go sightseeing. Plus, I take the boat out and fish most of the time. Some days I stay until dark. There's a good chance we won't even bump into each other at mealtimes."

Her face softened, though cautiously. "How do I get to the other islands to sightsee?"

Ah. He *was* tempting her. "I usually take one of my boats over, and most days I could drop you off before I go fishing, but if you want to go at odd times or want to come back early, I'll give you the number of my guy."

"You have a guy?"

"Yeah, he runs a boat service. Kind of like a car service with a boat. And the islands are great. You can visit a different one every day if you want. I have a couple of bikes. Take one and you can get around more easily."

Her eyes softened. "Wow." The sadness he sometimes heard in her voice dissolved into awe.

He motioned at the quiet, empty world around them. "It's a different way of living down here."

"I see that."

He laughed. "Trust me. You're going to love it. Plus, most of the vendors know me. So, I have accounts. If you need something like a tour guide, drop my name and they'll bill me."

Her chin lifted. "I'm not poor."

And here came the anger, the defensiveness. There were so many pieces to this puzzle that he simply couldn't dismiss it.

"Never said you were poor. Just offering you a chance to have some downtime." He headed inside to dress to go out on his boat and leave her alone to make her decision. "Choice is yours."

She debated the merits of staying for the whole five minutes it took to make toast and coffee. When she carried her breakfast outside to eat at one of the three round patio tables, the decision almost made itself. The peace of the area surrounded her. Looking out over the ocean, she felt one with the universe. Her tired brain began to revive, to remember all the reasons she should leave, but her body wouldn't let her. It wanted to walk on the beach, swim or tour his little island on one of the bikes.

After only a few seconds, her brain got on board. It began imagining the breeze blowing her hair as she rode a bike and drank in the scents of the foliage all around her.

She ate her toast and opted to give it a few hours. She could take a walk on the beach, explore the island on a bike and come back and swim. If he had returned from his fishing trip and she found him lounging around the pool, that would mean they'd be in each other's way and she'd call Dennis and leave.

But at least she'd have had one great, restful Sunday morning.

It made so much sense that she raced upstairs, slid into a bikini and put her list into action. When Cade hadn't returned after her swim, she took a nap.

It was past seven and she was upstairs in her suite when Cade finally entered the house. He didn't make a lot of noise, but he made enough that she knew he was downstairs. She heard the sound of a television but closed her suite door and silence reigned. She took a bottle of water out to the balcony off her room and watched the ocean for hours before she headed inside and fell asleep.

Monday morning, she woke feeling like a new woman. A day of exercise and sun must have been exactly what she needed. She slid into a swimsuit and a cover up and headed for the kitchen.

Unfortunately, when she reached the door, she saw Cade at the counter and stopped dead in her tracks. He wore a blue T-shirt over printed aqua shorts, bringing out the color of his eyes. One day of fishing on the water had turned his skin reddish brown. His yellow hair had begun to lighten.

"Good morning."

With his slight tan and disheveled hair, he

looked like he belonged here. On the beach. In the luxurious kitchen. Given that this was his house, she told herself that only made sense. She also told herself to be civil. Maybe even nice. He didn't have to let her stay. And she clearly needed the rest. Civility might get her another few days.

"Good morning."

He smiled briefly. "Given any thought to going into town sightseeing?"

She popped a pod into the coffee maker. Testing the waters to make sure he was still okay with this arrangement, she said, "Maybe tomorrow."

"Sounds good." He picked up his muffin and headed for the patio.

Relieved that he was so easygoing, she drank her coffee at the kitchen counter, reading the news on her phone. When she was finished, she cleared her dishes and headed outside to get a bike.

When she returned from her ride, he was on the beach. From the patio vantage point, she could see him edging his way into the water and eventually, when it got deep enough, diving in. She watched his muscular back work as he swam out into the waves and her heart skipped a beat, as memories poured through her.

Because spying on him, remembering their

past, wasn't part of the deal, she shrugged out of her cover-up, took a short swim in the pool and found a comfortable chaise. But even though she intended to read a book on her phone, her gaze kept rising to watch him swim. How casual he was. How comfortable. And the oddest thought hit her.

Was this what it was like to be a billionaire?

She almost asked him when he ambled up to the patio about an hour later. But she didn't want to talk to him. She most certainly didn't want to be curious about him.

He didn't say anything as he walked past her, into the house, but all her nerve endings tingled. Which—she told herself—was simply the weird feeling of living in a house with someone and not talking to them.

They didn't really know each other anymore. They both wanted a rest. The house was big enough for them both.

That was sort of their deal.

But when he came out at about three that afternoon and walked over to the big grill, he said, "I'm making steaks for dinner. Want one?"

She peered up at him over her sunglasses. Shirtless, still in his swim trunks, he casually dropped two steaks to the grill.

"Dinner? Now?"

"We don't eat on the clock here in paradise. We eat when we're hungry."

"But won't we get hungry again at night?"

He shrugged. The gorgeous muscles of his shoulders lifted. "Then we'll have a sandwich."

With the pool between them, she stared at his perfect back, the way his butt looked in the pale blue swimming trunks, then his long legs.

"You've gotten taller." The words spilled out even before she realized she was thinking them, and she could have bitten off her tongue. Their deal was no contact. But he started it when he brought out the steaks.

He looked over his shoulder at her. "You did too."

Relief rippled through her. Glad he didn't make a big deal out of her slip, she leaned back on the chaise.

"So rare, medium or well done?"

She sat up again. "Rare is good." Setting her phone on the small table by her chaise, she said, "Is there anything I can do?"

"Like?"

"Make a side dish? A salad?"

He shrugged again. "There's usually potato salad in the fridge."

He casually turned away and she stared at him. All those questions she'd had about him while watching him swim came tumbling back. He took for granted that everything he wanted would be at his fingertips.

"How do you know it's not old and spoiled?"

"The potato salad? I look at the use-by date. But, honestly, I call a service before I come down here. Things like steak are in the freezer, but the service comes in, inventories what's in the cabinets and refrigerator and updates everything."

"Wow."

He faced her with a frown. "Wow what?"

She glanced around. "I just... I don't know. It's all so perfect."

He snorted. "My life?"

She considered her answer for a second, trying to be neutral, but curiosity overwhelmed her and she said, "Yeah."

"It's not."

She rose from the chaise. "Now, don't be snooty. I didn't mean to insult you. But I've never even thought about what it would be like to have so much money I didn't have to work."

"I work!"

"Again, not trying to insult you. But I work, too, and I don't make nearly enough money to own an island."

"You could."

She laughed. She hadn't eaten lunch and the scent of the sizzling steaks lured her to the grill. Standing beside him, she said, "Not hardly. I have lots of customers in a three-or four-town area. But I'll never make a billion dollars."

"What if you franchised? What if you turned your idea into a business model that you could sell, then took the company public and cashed out?"

"Now you're just talking crazy."

"Not really. People make money three ways. From producing a good, providing a service or selling an idea. You could continue to provide the service, branch out, hire more people, go into more towns and earn a decent amount of money. But if you want to get rich, you have to provide all the stuff it takes for someone else to use your idea, then take a percentage of their proceeds."

"I know how franchising works. It's just not what I do. I'm a nurse with a business degree who likes her job just as it is."

"Then keep doing it."

"Seriously? After all those suggestions, you're telling me not to do anything?"

"Sometimes happiness and enjoying what you do is undervalued in our society. When I die, all the money I've accrued doesn't come with me. It actually becomes meaningless to me. Like I worked my life away for something that doesn't matter."

She gaped at him. "You hate your job?"

"No! I love my job." He took a breath. She saw a debate raging in his eyes before he said, "Mostly. There are some things that aren't easy—" He stopped again, drew another breath. "I'm just saying money's not the only measure of success. I think being happy is the greater measure."

He waited a beat, then said, "Are you happy?"

She didn't hesitate. She knew the wrong answer would cause him to probe. And she'd rather die than have him probe, digging around until he bumped into her secrets. "Yeah."

"Good. I'm glad."

Something about the way he said it warmed her heart. She'd felt uncomfortable about him for so long that it was nice to have positive feelings for him.

He chuckled. "I'll even give you the island once a year for a vacation."

"I told you. I'm not a charity case."

"When a friend lets a friend use his island, it's not about charity. It's about sharing. Don't you share?"

"Sure. I just never thought of billionaires as being people who share."

"Why wouldn't we? We're the ones with the best toys."

She laughed. Again. And for the first time since she'd broken up with him, she missed him. Her heart filled with a yearning so profound her breathing stopped. As much as the feeling nudged her to recognize staying might not be a good idea, it also made her long for time with him. Her common sense warned her that might be the worst decision of her life, but she just wanted to spend a couple of days in the pure, innocent happiness they'd shared as kids—even though she knew it wasn't possible. She was different now. Damaged. Plus, they couldn't have what they'd talked about as two teenagers planning a future.

She could never forget that.

But her yearning wasn't about the future. It was about now. What they could have now. Maybe if she didn't push too hard, didn't want too much, these next few days would satisfy the little ache in her chest that popped up every time she looked at him. Wouldn't it be fun to get to know him again? To laugh? To be silly?

She considered again that that might not be smart, but she silenced her usually wise brain.

Just for once, she didn't want to think about tomorrow, about consequences, about any damned thing except having some fun.

CHAPTER FIVE

THEY ATE THEIR steaks with the potato salad
Reese found in the refrigerator, just as Cade
had told her she would. When their meal ended,
they went their separate ways. He actually took
a short nap and woke when she returned from
a walk on the beach and plopped on the chaise
beside his, surprising him.

With the lazy, late afternoon sun shining
down on them, it felt so damned right for her to
be next to him that it seemed as if no time had
passed between that summer twelve years ago
and this minute. Different pool. Same people.

Happiness stuttered through him and he sat
up. "Hey, you know what we need?"

She peered at him over her sunglasses.
"What?"

"No-bakes."

"The cookies?"

He nodded.

She laughed. "Seriously, you're hungry?"

"No. I just want a treat."

She lifted herself off her chaise. "If you have the right things in the kitchen, I can make them. But I think I want to shower first. I'm all sweaty from my walk."

He sat up. "Write down what you need, and I'll check the cupboards while you're showering."

She headed inside. "Sounds like a plan."

When she reached the kitchen, she grabbed the notepad and pencil attached to the refrigerator by a magnet. "Let's see... Sugar, butter, vanilla, milk..."

He ambled up to the center island. "I know we have those."

"That leaves oatmeal and cocoa powder."

"Cocoa powder?"

"Yeah. It's how cooks make things chocolate. Until you add the cocoa, brownies are blondies." She frowned. "You might not have it."

"You'd be surprised what the shopping service stocks."

She pulled away from the center island. "Okay. See you in about half an hour."

"Make it forty-five minutes."

Almost out of the kitchen, she turned and frowned at him. "What?"

"Just... Nothing." He laughed. "Go shower."

She left the room, and he didn't even bother looking in the cupboards. He wasn't a fan of oatmeal, so he was sure his service didn't stock it. Cocoa powder? He sincerely doubted they provided that either.

But he wanted the no-bake cookies. He liked the feeling of him and Reese behaving normally. Their inconsequential chitchat while grilling their steaks had taken away his brain's need to go over Roger's accident again and again and again. And having her plop down beside him was just…nice.

He would be careful. He would be honest. But he wouldn't argue with something that was working.

He picked up his phone and called Dennis. He told him to bring a box of oatmeal and cocoa powder.

Dennis laughed and said, "I'll ask my wife."

Cade agreed that was a good idea. "Don't take too long. Reese is showering. I need the stuff to be here when she's out."

Dennis said, "Got it!"

Cade disconnected the call, then he pulled the rest of the items Reese said she needed, set them on the big center island and walked out to the pool. In forty minutes, he heard the sound of the helicopter. In another ten, he heard the noise of Dennis riding one of the bikes up to the house. He got out of the pool, dried off and entered the kitchen the same time Dennis did.

He set a bag on the table. "My wife says these are what you want."

"What who wants?"

Seeing Reese in the doorway, Cade winced. "We didn't have the cocoa powder."

She peeked in the bag. "Or the oatmeal."

"And now we do," Cade said happily, trying to make light of the fact that he'd just spent a thousand dollars to get some cookies. He didn't give a damn. Dennis loved it when he did this kind of thing because the money was good. But he had a sneaking feeling Reese would not understand.

She surprised him by saying a pleasant goodbye to Dennis when he left and immediately started to stir ingredients into a heavy pan.

She took a quick breath and glanced up at him. "What would you have done if we didn't have the right pan?"

He peered at her. "The right pan?"

"It takes a thick, sturdy pan to cook the sugar and butter together. If it's too thin, the paste burns. So, what would you have done if we hadn't had this pan?"

He shrugged. "I don't know."

"Would you have sent Dennis to a big-box store, looking for pans?"

"Because we have the pan, it's irrelevant."

"Not really. It's all tied up in you being a

billionaire." She shook her head. "Holy crap, your life is different."

He couldn't tell if she liked that. Still, if something about him had made her ditch him when he was eighteen, being different should be a good thing.

But he didn't want to risk it. He didn't want to risk whatever this feeling was that kept rolling through the air, capturing his heart, taking him back to the happiest time of his life. Not when he desperately needed something else to think about other than the worry that he'd made a mistake, that the safety protocols he'd approved hadn't been enough, and it was his fault that a man had died.

Was it so wrong that his poor brain wanted a rest?

If stopping conversations that might make her mad kept her here, then that's what he'd do. He grabbed a beer from the fridge and walked toward the open doorway that connected the living room to the outside. "I'm going to take a swim."

Focused on making sure the sugar and butter didn't burn as they reached the right temperature and consistency, Reese barely noticed he was gone. But when she measured the cocoa to stir it in, she paused.

God only knew how much money it had cost him to get the cocoa.

The truth of his wealth, his life, rippled through her. He was the same, but different. He'd always been a cut above the rest of the kids in their group. Strong enough to deal with his parents, he'd had substance that high school kids normally didn't have.

Her heart squeezed, then swelled with longing for all the things they'd lost. All the things they seemed to be finding again—

Gut-wrenching sorrow filled her so quickly, her brain wasn't fast enough to compartmentalize it. They couldn't "find" anything again. The dreams they had as teenagers weren't possible. Not only had a rape changed her, but she couldn't have kids.

She took a breath. *This* was exactly why she shouldn't be around Cade. She'd had her life under control for years and now suddenly everything wrong was closing in on her.

Because seeing him had her focusing on the past.

She frowned at the thought that had crept into her brain. Part of moving on had been learning to let go of the past. To use her thoughts to plan the future. To actually be present with people. If she didn't want to remember everything wrong in her life—and given that she and Cade didn't have a future—the trick to enjoying this week would be focusing on the present.

Maybe that was why her brain had kept making her curious? It knew the way to stop thinking about the past was to direct all conversations to the present, to who he was now. Or maybe to how he'd become who he was now?

After adding oatmeal to the hot batter, she found parchment paper, scooped out spoonfuls of fudgy batter and dropped them onto the paper to cool. She'd always thought Cade would stay in town to take care of his crazy parents. Instead, he'd opted for a university too far away to commute and never came home. Not even for holidays. She supposed work necessitated he settle in Manhattan with his friends. Which was lucky because he'd ended up wealthy.

But how had he met the two friends?

And how had they known forming a team would work?

There was a story there and for the first time in over a decade she had the chance to hear it. She'd loved him with every fiber of her being. How could she not want to hear how he'd reached his dreams?

She poured two glasses of milk and carried

them out to the patio. "Now you've done it. I'm curious."

He rose from the chaise, took the glasses from her hands and set them on one of the round tables. "About?"

"You. For Pete's sake. We were two normal small-town kids. We went to the same school. Rooted for the local football team. Got ice cream at the Windmill. Honestly, if you'd asked me when we were dating, I would have guessed I'd be the one to leave and you'd be the one to stay."

"To take care of my crazy parents?"

"Yes!"

"Did they need me?"

She pondered that. "No. Once you were gone, they sorted everything out. After their divorce, they never talked to each other, but it didn't matter. Everything had been settled. Divided. There was no reason for them to talk. No reason to fight."

"I rest my case."

She gaped at him. "You left to force them to settle things on their own?"

"No. I wanted a good education. Having them finally settle their divorce was an unexpected perk. Like leaving them had killed two birds with one stone."

"Huh." She let all that rumble through her mind.

"What about you? Why didn't *you* leave?"

Safety and protection. Routine and family.

None of which she could tell him. Once she began opening those doors, it would be only a few steps before she told him her secrets.

And then what?

And then nothing!

He couldn't change facts any more than she could. Plus, she wanted this week to be relaxing. Not a rehash of her pain.

"Cookies will be cool enough to eat in about ten minutes."

He laughed. "Come on. I'm not asking for nuclear launch codes. You can tell me why you didn't leave. I won't judge. I swear. No judgment here."

She sighed, scrambling for a way to satisfy him without even brushing up against her secrets. "It was me being sappy. You know?" She shrugged. "I didn't leave because I wanted to be around my family."

"Why didn't you just say that? You always loved your family." He rolled his eyes. "You certainly loved them more than I loved mine. In a way, your normal family gave me hope that there were regular people in the world while my parents spewed hatred and threw things." He shook his head. "Wow. That was a weird year."

He didn't know the half of it, and she suddenly felt a tiny nudge of guilt for not being totally honest with him, but that was for the best. They had a few days together. There was no place for deep, dark secrets. No time for anything serious.

Her voice soft, she said, "Yes. It was a weird year."

"Don't feel bad that you didn't leave town to find fame and fortune."

Her teenage dreams poured into her head. She'd wanted to move to Washington, DC, to work for a congressman and do important things. Another thing Finn had stolen from her.

"I never wanted fame and fortune. I wanted to help people."

"You *do* help people. Being a nurse is the very definition of helping people."

She said, "Yeah, I guess."

"No guessing about it. You've gotten my dad to do a billion things he'd never have done on his own."

She glanced down at the stone floor of the patio. "Stretching your dad is *not* how I saw myself helping people."

He sobered. "No. Probably not." He was quiet for a few seconds, then he grinned. "Wanna stop talking and go back to pretending we're kids again?"

She caught his gaze. Connection wove through her. He might be older, but he was still Cade. Fun-loving, easygoing Cade. The guy she'd loved. And maybe that was why she wanted this time with him? Because he could be silly. He could be carefree. Fun.

"Was that what we were doing?"

"Sort of. Remember how I'd grill something we'd eat for lunch, then beg you to make no-bakes?"

The recollection of those afternoons was inconsequential. Simple. Because they'd been two normal teens with working parents entertaining themselves. "Yes."

"Except we never sat around and waited for the cookies to cool."

She laughed and swatted his arm. "We never ate them hot!"

"No." He angled his thumb at the blue water behind him. "We'd wait in the pool."

She pointed at her yellow T-shirt. "I'm not wearing a swimsuit."

"Since when did that stop us?"

More memories flooded her. Swimming in street clothes. Swimming in their underwear. Swimming without any clothes at all.

He took a step closer. "You could swim in that T-shirt and those shorts, but there were times we swam without clothes. Remember?"

She did. Heat and need roared through her. Back then, he would have easily grabbed the hem of her T-shirt and yanked it over her head, and she would have giggled with delight before they both jumped into the cool blue water.

The memory, so sweet and so pure, filled her with such yearning that she had to swallow before she could say, "I'm not that girl anymore."

He stepped back, away from her. "Well, I'm still that guy. Plus, I'm wearing my trunks. So, I will swim while the cookies cool."

He leaped into the water and did the butterfly stroke, bobbing up and down as his body cut through the waves his dive had made.

Her head tilted as she watched him, but the strangest realization took her attention. *He hadn't tried to change her mind.* Younger Cade wouldn't have let her stand by the pool while he swam. He would have found a way to get her into the water.

She could think he really had changed, but realized he'd simply grown up. He wasn't the hyper, happy guy she'd fallen for, the kid with the off-the-wall parents who felt he had to control everything. He was—

Better?

Himself…but better?

Another unexpected thought hit her. She liked grown-up Cade a hundred times more than eighteen-year-old Cade. Not that eighteen-year-old Cade wasn't fun. He was. He was silly and playful and there were days she simply could not get enough of him. But eighteen-year-old Cade had needed all kinds of assurances. With his parents doing embarrassing things and his being called to referee, he'd needed to know his parents' antics didn't bother her. He'd always needed to know she didn't think him crazy by association.

This older, more confident version didn't have those needs.

He was fine.

She glanced at him swimming. He *was* fine. He was very, very fine.

And they had been having fun until she'd ended it by refusing to go into the pool.

Maybe she should stop being the stick-in-the-mud?

If he was willing to set aside their past and play for the few days they had together, maybe she should stop shutting things down when he made suggestions that surprised her?

After all, she was the one who didn't want to revisit the past.

And she did want to relax. Have some fun. Innocent fun.

Realizing just how much fun they could have, she laughed. But as she turned back to the kitchen, a memory of their first date flashed in her brain—

He'd taken her to the movies, then the Windmill, the ice-cream stand in the center of their small town, with picnic tables where friends frequently gathered. People from her group had mingled with people from his. They were noisy, silly kids having fun. The mood was light when he drove her home and walked her to her door.

But when they stopped under the glow of the porch light, the way he looked at her told her that for him this was so much more, and she realized it was for her too. When he bent his head and touched his lips to hers, her heart had stuttered and something deep inside her exploded. Young and foolish, she'd believed she'd found "the one."

The kiss deepened. Their tongues twined like they'd kissed a million times before. Need crackled through her. Emotions she'd only read about in books found meaning.

They finally broke apart and just stared at each other for a few seconds. Then he grinned.

"Good night."

Her voice shivered when she said, "Good night."

He all but skipped down the sidewalk to his

car and her heart swelled to capacity with real love—

Her breath stuttered, bringing her back to reality. She had been the craziest combination of happy and scared. But she'd been smart enough to know what she wanted and let things happen between them.

Would it really be possible for *her* to let go of all her inhibitions—her *rules*—her past—and just have fun the way they used to?

In the bubble of this island? Where nothing they did mattered?

Yes. It would. She would love to let her guard down and sink into the feelings that wanted to overwhelm her. To enjoy herself. Enjoy *him.*

The question was how?

CHAPTER SIX

CADE'S OLD SIXTH sense about cooling cookies returned easily and he was out of the pool and drying off when Reese returned to the patio with them.

He pointed at a small table between two chaise lounges. "Put them here." He tossed his towel to a chair and picked up the glasses of milk she'd brought out a few minutes before. He set them beside the cookies, then he lowered himself to a chaise and she cautiously lowered herself to the one beside it.

They ate their cookies in total silence. Curiosity about her nagged at him—especially her cautious streak. But for as much as he wanted to know everything about her, he was afraid to ask. Questions were hard. Answers were sometimes harder. He didn't want to offend her and have her leave. He wanted this time with her.

Fudgy cookie number two disappeared into his mouth. He took a drink of milk. She took a sip of milk. He grabbed another cookie. She settled into the chaise.

Awkwardness filled the air. It didn't seem right not to talk. But he couldn't risk forcing things.

She ate her second cookie in silence, and he knew if he didn't think of something quickly, she'd retreat to her room again.

Suddenly, the perfect idea came to him. "Hey! Let's take the boat out."

She peeked at him. "You're going to fish?"

"No. But you'll want to go to the other islands sometime. Let's head out now and I'll show you how easy it is to get there."

She thought about that, then sat up. "Can we get back before dark?"

"It's spring, remember? Lots of daylight left."

"Okay, then let's go."

Relief slithered through him. "Okay. Let's go."

He ducked into the T-shirt he had tossed to one of the patio chairs and slipped into his sandals while she found her tennis shoes. Then he led her down the path cut out of the thick foliage to his dock. His fishing boat bobbed on one side of the row of wooden planks that kept the vehicles loosely moored. The other side held his cabin cruiser. Not so big as to be braggy, but big enough to take a pretty girl out onto the water, the white boat sparkled in the sun.

She ambled up to it. "Nice."

"Expensive." He waved around the island. "All of this comes at a price. But it's what gives me peace. A retreat."

"I remember you wanted a place to run away to when your parents did crazy things."

He laughed. "Yep. This is it."

"I like it."

"I do too." He also liked that the awkwardness between them had disappeared again.

He helped her aboard and pointed to the steering area. "That, of course, is how we navigate. There's a tiny kitchenette and sleeping space below deck. Over there is where people lay out in the sun."

"Very nice."

He shouldn't have needed her approval, and he supposed he didn't, but it felt good. Solid. Right. Like another step in making things natural between them.

He lifted the lid on one of the storage compartments that served as a bench seat. "Want a life jacket?"

She looked out at all the water, then laughed. "Yes."

He pulled one out and tossed it to her. "Here you go."

She slid into the vest easily but fumbled with the catches. He reached over and snapped them like the pro that he was, but his fingers skimmed her arms, chest and stomach sending nerves scurrying through him. They'd been as close as two people could be. When he touched her, a unique kind of energy filled him, and now they were supposed to be friends?

They had to be. He wanted to know why she'd dumped him. He wanted closure. But he'd give that up if they could be friends. Real friends, the way they had been. They'd been so close that he simply could not believe they were meant to dislike each other. They'd always had something special, and though they might not be lovers again, they could at least be friends.

He pulled away from her and headed to the helm, but her confused voice stopped him. "You're not wearing a life vest?"

"I don't need one. I swim like a fish."

"What if you get knocked unconscious?"

He turned to her with a chuckle. "Are you going to knock me unconscious?"

"No, but you could fall out of the boat and hit your head."

He frowned.

"Think this through. You get knocked out

and sink like a stone. I can swim, but I'm not sure I can lug your body back to the boat."

"When did you get to be such a chicken?"

He asked the question as a joke, but Rule Number Seven, *Control the things you can control*, popped into her head. She wasn't exactly obsessive-compulsive about it, but she looked ahead to trouble and, if there was a way, stopped it.

Still, she wanted to drop her vigilance with him and have fun. He was letting his guard down. She could see that in everything he said, the way he kept trying to smooth things over. She could do it too. One step at a time.

She sucked in a breath. "I'm not a chicken. Just careful."

"Seriously, you used to have a daring streak that made me proud."

"Things change."

Hte looked ready to question her again, or maybe argue about the protective gear, but he sighed and wrestled himself into the life jacket. "Satisfied?"

The happiness she felt around more mature Cade filled her. She didn't exactly want him to be a different person. She'd loved eighteen-year-old Cade with passion and innocence. But the maturity he kept showing relaxed her, pushed her rules to the back of her brain, made her believe that eventually she would let go and have real fun with him. Not to risk her heart. Not to fall in love. Just to have a happy time together.

"Actually, yes. I am satisfied."

He grunted and headed to the other side of the boat. Walking past the steering wheel and what she assumed to be navigational equipment, he lifted the padded seat and revealed a cooler of beer. "Want one?"

She hadn't quite been able to bring herself to drink beer, but things were working out so well that having a drink together was just another step. "I don't suppose you have any wine."

"I do." He pulled out a beer for himself, set it on the padded seat and disappeared below deck. When he reappeared, he surprised her with a container of wine that looked like a juice box.

She took it. "Handy."

"This *is* a boat. Though I have glasses in the kitchenette, boxes are easier."

He motioned for her to follow him to what she considered the front of the vehicle. He explained the navigational tools, especially the safety protocols, relaxing her even more. Then he started the engine with the press of a button and took them out on the blue water.

She leaned back on the bench seat and closed

her eyes, enjoying the rush of the wind as the boat plowed out into open sea. "This is great."

"I know," he called as he navigated the boat farther and farther out until, when she opened her eyes, she saw nothing but water.

"Wow."

He turned off the engine and sat beside her on the bench. Leaning back, he angled his feet on a convenient storage space.

"Do you see why I like relaxing on this?"

"Yeah. Though I'm not sure why a billion-aire needs to relax."

He snorted. "You don't think responsibility for tons of money is stressful?"

"I think having tons of money looks like fun."

"How about having responsibility for ten thousand employees?"

She winced. "That's a lot of people."

"I am aware."

"And it would be stressful."

He looked down, studying his beer can. "We lost someone the day before my dad had his stroke."

She blinked. With the way their conversations had all been so light and easy, that was the last thing she'd expected him to say. "Lost someone?"

"At a warehouse. Guy was driving a forklift. He drove into a concrete wall."

Her heart skipped a beat as the eighteen-year-old Cade she remembered meshed with the mature adult, and she knew how hard that had to be for him.

She stared at the angles and planes of his handsome face, though he stared down at the hands holding his beer can and wouldn't look at her.

"I'm so sorry."

"Everyone thinks being in charge of insurance is boring. But that also puts me in charge of safety protocols."

"You blame yourself?"

He peered up at her. "No. But, yes."

She knew that feeling, that odd, unfair guilt after being raped. When she wondered what she should have done. What she could have done. What she hadn't seen. What she should have recognized.

She took a breath, thinking of eighteen-year-old Cade again. Wondering what she would have said to him. Simple understanding won. "I get that."

"You do?"

"Yeah." She really did. The connection she had felt with him trembled through her. Scary at first, then suddenly as natural as breathing. They'd always been on the same page. Always clicked. Though she didn't have guts enough to tell him about her rape, she did comprehend his anguish. "In nursing, we're responsible for patients in a way doctors aren't. We recognize that day-to-day little stuff counts. Even if no one sees it, I go the extra mile. Look for things other people don't. When something goes wrong, I take it apart like a jigsaw puzzle until I figure out why."

"My partners were understanding to a point. But they're not the ones responsible for making sure everyone is safe."

"True, but your case is different. Sometimes in life accidents just happen. There are some things no one can control." That had been the stumbling block in her recovery from Finn's attack. It wasn't an accident. There had been lots of blame to go around. Finn for getting drunk. His parents for not being responsible with the refrigerator of beer in their garage. Her for not thinking ahead, not recognizing the potential danger. But in therapy she'd realized that as long as you were placing blame, you couldn't heal.

"The thing is," she began slowly, not sure what she was going to say, but knowing the reasoning she wanted to get across. "You need some time to read the accident reports, figure out if there were things that could have been done to prevent it. Then implement those things. And do better."

Cade examined her face for a few seconds, not sure why the need to talk had pushed him, except she'd been the person he'd turned to in the last pivotal place in his life, his parents' divorce. And here she was again.

As crazy as it sounded, their connection was still there. She was as street smart, as full of common sense, as she'd been all those years ago. Talking about this with her fit the mood, the moment, the problem he was having.

And maybe even explained why he hadn't wanted her to leave. Deep down in his subconscious he'd known they'd come to this.

"They're doing an autopsy. The guy was older. The way it looked, he drove into the wall full force. Coroner said he might have had a heart attack or an episode of some sort. Maybe a seizure." He took a breath. "The forklift is also being examined. There could have been a mechanical failure." He shrugged. "It wouldn't change the company's responsibility to his family, but it would explain things."

"And make you feel better?"

"No. It would be another piece of the picture. I don't think there's a way for me to feel better. Having an accident that resulted in a death was a shock. But as you said, I can do better." He took a breath. "One thing I've learned over the years is every job you have trains you for the next one."

She nodded. "True. But I'm still sorry this happened."

He drew another breath, this one longer, needing a second to compose himself. Emotion over the accident flooded him, but so did an overwhelming surge of gratitude at having her here, listening, sharing his grief.

"Yeah. So am I."

They leaned back on the bench seat again, resting against the boat. He'd said his piece. She'd listened and offered some wisdom that helped his brain settle down. Now it was time to move on.

He glanced sideways at her. "Wanna swim?"

"God, no! Not with fish!"

"You are such a coward! Where's the girl I loved—"

His heart thumped. He hadn't meant to say that, to remind her that he'd loved her, but it slipped out. And he suddenly realized he stood by it. He had loved her, and he'd loved her because of what had happened between them just now. He could talk to her. Easily. Naturally.

Their gazes caught and held. Her eyes softened and filled with a million longings, but she quickly looked away. "We should probably get back."

And there she was again. Strong Reese. The girl he'd confided in—except stronger somehow. She didn't merely know what to say. She knew when to pull back, move on.

"You might have turned into a coward—"

She snorted.

"—but you're awfully smart. I can hear it in almost every word that comes out of your mouth. What happened that made you so smart?"

She leaned forward, pretending to adjust the shoestring of her tennis shoe. "Why do you think something happened? Maybe I just paid attention in school."

He shook his head. "The best learning comes by experience."

"Well, look at you, getting all philosophical."

"And look at you, evading my question. *Again.*"

She shrugged. "Because I think my story is a story for another time."

He leaned down to peer into her face. "So, there is a story?"

She held his gaze for a few moments and finally said, "Yes."

"And you'll talk about it eventually?"

She shrugged. "If we talk about everything that happened in the past twelve years, we're going to need more than a week on your island."

The way she so casually said she'd be staying the week stopped his heart. He might have needed her to hang around for a diversion and a chance to get an explanation on why she'd dumped him, but now they were having fun. Being friends. The way they had been when they were younger. He simply did not want that to end.

He'd already realized when he pushed too hard, she clammed up. Having her say she'd stay the whole week had to be enough for now.

They sat for a few minutes while he finished his beer, then he rose, walked back to the helm and started the boat again. He took them toward the islands, and as they breezed past the chain that made up the Florida Keys, he pointed out the bigger ones, the ones not privately owned, where shops and homes created colorful streets and boat docks frequently became block parties.

He watched the wind ruffle her hair but was more taken by the smile on her face. Even Trace, who loved boats as much as Cade did, was never as happy as she was with the wind in her hair and the setting sun winking at them.

Corresponding happiness cascaded through him, as the phone in the pocket of his swimming trunks buzzed. He casually slid it out, saw the call was from his father and clicked Refuse Call. He wasn't quite ready to talk to the old coot yet—

How could he be angry with his dad for setting them up this way?

Not only had they quickly gotten past the initial, confusing anger and awkwardness, but she'd been exactly the person to talk to about the accident at the warehouse.

He glanced back at Reese and she grinned at him. His heart filled and he returned her smile, unable to stop the suspicion that his new and improved dad might know something he didn't know.

Maybe Reese had said something to Martin when she'd been playing Yahtzee and Uno with him the past week?

Pleasure filled him. Just the thought that she'd told his dad that she'd loved the year she'd spent with Cade, or maybe that she missed him or maybe even that she was sorry she'd broken up with him, sent his brain in a million different directions.

But mostly, it changed his feelings about this trip, about what it might mean.

As he helped her onto the dock at his island, he told himself not to let his thoughts go too far. She was happy. He was happy. He shouldn't make a big deal out of it and want more.

They started up the darkening path to his house, but her steps wobbled and he caught her hand. Electricity sizzled through him. "There are lights that will turn on soon. Just let me hang on to you until they do."

"Okay."

Her soft, breathless voice intensified the electricity.

"I didn't pave this path because I sort of like the natural feel of the island."

"Makes sense."

"Now I wish I had."

She laughed. "Don't be silly. As you said, the lights will come on in a minute."

They didn't. Cade held her hand the entire way from the dock to the infinity pool.

When he should have let go, awkwardness stopped him. Standing on the patio in the moonlight, holding the hand of the first woman he'd loved, he almost groaned.

He should have just dropped her hand when it would have been a natural, easy thing to do! Now he was caught in a weird place between the past and the present and it was as confusing as it was filled with promise.

She glanced up at him with a soft smile. "I could use my hand back."

He sniffed. "Yeah. Sorry."

But he still held on to her hand, as that warm, wonderful sense of potential rippled through him. If she'd told his dad she was sorry she'd broken up with him, if she'd missed him—

Everything he believed about their past would be different.

Of course, if she'd said something while he was still at Harvard, he wouldn't have married a woman who'd caused him to decide marriage was for chumps and to vow that he'd never fall into that trap again. He would have stayed in their small town and joined his dad's investment firm. He would have been...happy.

That wasn't quite right. He was happy now. How could he not be?

He frowned. He might be happy, but he was also standoffish and suspicious.

If he and Reese had stayed together, he might not have billions of dollars but he would still be wealthy. And he'd also have her. Have her laughter and homespun wisdom to mix with his intelligence. Together they would have been unstoppable—

He needed to know. If she'd said something to his dad, regretted breaking up with him, missed him even a little bit, he needed to know. And there might be a simple way to find out.

With an easy nudge on her hand to bring her closer, he lowered his head and pressed his lips to hers. Tentatively. Almost like asking a question.

She stiffened at first and he thought she'd

pull back, but as quickly as she'd stiffened, she softened, then stepped closer.

It was all the invitation he needed. He wrapped both arms around her and she slid her hands to his shoulders.

Their lips met in a joyful reunion of souls, pressing and nibbling at first, then opening to pure bliss. Happiness exploded, along with caution.

No matter what might have been, she had hurt him.

Twelve years had passed.

They were both different.

They could never re-create what might have been.

He felt that in their kiss. The ease, the simplicity, where there had once been teenage passion.

And he was old enough, smart enough to think this through before he did something he'd regret.

He pulled back, took a breath and smiled at her. "Good night."

Their gazes locked, she said, "Good night," before heading into the house.

He watched her, the full moon glistening off the water in his pool, the sounds of the ocean rhythmically lapping at the shore.

That hadn't been the kiss of two former lovers. It was something new. Something different.

Which could be for the best.

Or not.

He might have been telling her bits and pieces about what had happened in the twelve years that had passed since they'd seen each other, but she didn't know the big things, the personal things. Like a divorce that had ravaged his soul and made him cautious about relationships—forget another marriage. She didn't know about the connection he'd made with Wyatt and Trace, two men who felt more like brothers than business partners.

And he didn't know a damned thing about what had happened to her.

When he asked, she evaded. Always.

Which could mean she was hiding something important.

Something she didn't want him to know.

He had billions of dollars. Assets he had to protect. A heart that had been shattered and a soul that was only beginning to recover. He might like her, but pretty soon she was going to have to spill the secret she so clearly was hiding.

Or he'd have to step back and return to the strangers-sharing-the-same-house suggestion he'd made when he'd first asked her to stay.

CHAPTER SEVEN

REESE NEVER SLEPT as well as she did that night. It might have been the fresh sea air, but something cleared her head and tired her body enough that sleep had come easily and lasted until rays of sunlight drifted into her bedroom, waking her—

She jerked up in bed.

He'd kissed her.

Not like eighteen-year-old Cade. Like the mature adult she knew he was.

Joy flooded her. Yearnings morphed into possibilities.

She squeezed her eyes shut. Common sense told her to stop the hope before it turned into something that couldn't happen. It was one thing to have fun and do things together and enjoy their time on the island, quite another to start something. Like a relationship—

Oh, Lord. They could not have a relationship. She had to talk with Cade and tell him she wasn't interested, but her happy heart and her bewitched soul did not listen. She and Cade had connected when they'd talked. But, even better, he hadn't pushed her. Waiting for the cookies to cool, she'd refused to swim with him. He'd swum on his own. She'd refused to tell him her story. He'd accepted it. The more he accepted, the less he pushed, the more she trusted him.

And just because he kissed her, it did not mean he was leading them to something serious. He could want what she did.

Some fun. To enjoy the few days they had left on the island.

Maybe the kiss hadn't been a surprise? Maybe it had been a logical next step? Not to something permanent. But a step to expressing what they were feeling in the moment. If she didn't try to define it, it could lead to something wonderful. A deeper, more fun few days than time spent swimming or on a boat.

Satisfied with that conclusion, she slipped out of bed.

So now what?

Needing coffee before she could think this through, she quickly dressed in yoga pants and a T-shirt and headed for the kitchen. Cade sat at the center island, staring at his phone.

She could be a coward, turn and go back

to her room to wait until he was gone. Or she could be the mature woman she was, go into the kitchen and see what happened.

Stepping into the room, she said, "Good morning."

Instead of saying good morning, Cade lifted his phone. "Here she is now."

The faces of two men took up the entire screen. One said, "Hey." The other said, "So you're Reese."

Confused, she continued her walk to the coffeemaker, quietly saying, "Yes, I'm Reese. Good morning."

She heard one of the guys say, "Shy?"

"No. I think she's one of those people who need coffee before she wakes up." Cade glanced over at her. "Do you want to drink your coffee outside or in here."

"Outside?"

"Okay. I'll stay inside. You go outside." He turned his phone to her again. "The guy with the glasses is Trace. Guy with the beard and the baby is Wyatt. My business partners."

She waved uncomfortably and said, "Nice to meet you," but his consideration both with giving her the choice of outside or in, and introducing her to his partners, increased the feeling that she could trust him.

She made her coffee listening to him talk to

his friends about their business, then took the big mug outside, lowered herself to a chaise and stared at the beautiful blue sea.

Twenty minutes later when her coffee was gone and she was about to plan her day in her head, Cade came out of the kitchen and plopped down on the chaise beside hers.

"They think you're beautiful."

The silly, bubbly sensation she had when she woke returned. The way she felt about him had changed so fast it should scare her. She should be packing her bags and calling Dennis. But they had what was left of a week. Not the rest of her life. They'd always had fun together. Now he was proving she could trust him.

There was no need to run. Not when she so desperately needed some fun in her life.

He frowned. "You don't know that you're beautiful?"

She smiled at him. "I'm normal. Average-looking at best."

He shook his head. "No. You're beautiful. You have that whole red hair, green eyes spitfire thing going on."

Pleasure rippled through her and she knew she wanted to stay for more than a little fun. She'd missed him. Missed their connection. It didn't matter that anything that happened between them would be only a vacation fling.

She didn't want forever. He probably wasn't thinking about forever either.

Still, the best way to make sure things didn't get out of hand would be to manage the amount of time they spent together.

She said, "You're crazy," and rose from her chair. "I think I'll take a bike ride."

He smiled and lay back on the chaise. "Okay."

Relief filled her. Once again, he hadn't pushed. She walked into the house, ran up the steps to her bedroom, slipped into a bathing suit, then put on a big T-shirt over her suit and headed off. She took a ride around the island, and the feeling of control intensified.

He was an adult. So was she. They were friends. Had been lovers. They finally had a chance to see each other again. It was not wrong to want to enjoy that. He wasn't pushing. If something happened, it would happen naturally—

And she wanted it.

She rode the bike up to the front of the house, then rolled it into the garage before entering the quiet foyer. Realizing Cade was probably fishing, she ambled through the main room to the open doors for the patio, stripping off her T-shirt so she could jump into the pool.

But as she lifted her foot to step outside, a woman said, "He left you a note."

Her heart about jumped out of her chest. She pressed her hand to it as she turned to see a tall blond woman standing by the big center island in the kitchen.

"You scared the crap out of me." She took a breath, calming herself, knowing an intruder wouldn't tell her Cade had left her a note. Would she?

"Who are you?"

"Nina, the maid. I'm here Tuesdays. Cade forgot. I surprised him too." She waited a beat, then repeated, "He left you a note."

"Okay." She turned toward the kitchen.

"Never seen him leave anybody a note."

Not sure what to say, Reese only smiled. She got the implication. It was unusual for Cade to leave a note, so Nina the housekeeper was wondering about their relationship. She was in good company because Reese had no idea herself.

She glanced down at the note.

Gone fishing.
Hope you're having fun without me.

Her heart stuttered and all the emotions of being a teenager desperately in love poured through her. That was what he used to say when she took an afternoon to be with her friends. The memory of the intensity of his feelings back then automatically brought joy to her soul, but little warning bells tinkled in her brain.

Since her arrival on the island, she'd had moments when it felt like they'd gone back in time and were picking up where they left off, but she hadn't taken them seriously. What if Cade had?

Worry tightened her chest. Back then, they'd been two naive kids, planning a future together with careers, marriage and kids.

Kids.

Her breath stuttered. Surely, he didn't see them picking up where they'd left off, resurrecting dreams...reviving that future?

He couldn't. It was unrealistic. And he was smart. Too smart to think something so wrong.

She told herself she'd made too much of a stupid note and headed over to the open doors again, slightly annoyed that Nina kept watching her. As she finished tidying up the kitchen and the living area, her gaze strayed to Reese as if she were some sort of anomaly.

When the maid was gone, Reese forced herself to forget the odd way Nina had watched her and the fact that Cade leaving her a note had meant something. He liked her enough to tell her where he was so she wouldn't worry.

It was nice…sweet even. And a good sign that he had feelings for her beyond housemate.

All that was positive. She would not make more of it than that.

When he returned from fishing at five, she closed the book app on her phone and set it on the small table beside the chaise.

"Catch anything?"

She also wouldn't let herself feel nervous around him. They'd kissed. They'd built trust. They were back to being friends. She was on board with a vacation romance. The next move was his.

"I catch things. I just can't always use everything I hook so I give it away. Gave a tuna to the people two islands down."

"You gave away a tuna? I love tuna!"

He shrugged. "Thought we'd go out to dinner tonight."

Though he'd tried to be casual, she realized he was making "the" move. This was a date. He was asking her out.

Her heart thrummed. For once in her life, what she wanted, what she'd envisioned was actually happening.

Except—

"I didn't really bring the kind of clothes a person would wear to a restaurant."

He laughed. "This is Florida. If you have shorts, a decent shirt and flip-flops, you're golden."

Happiness filled her. She was going on a date! Not with the kid from her memories of being sixteen, but the guy he was right now. A golden-haired Adonis with a sharp mind and a sense of humor, who loved cookies.

"I'll need fifteen minutes to change."

"You've got more like an hour. Unless you'd like to spend some time touring the island before we eat."

"You made a reservation?"

"Guilty."

She shook her head. "Pretty sure of yourself."

He glanced around. "Competition's limited here on Cade Island. Thought the odds were on my side."

She groaned at his bad joke. "All right. I'll take the whole hour and make good use of it."

With the extra time, she fixed her hair and applied makeup. She might be wearing shorts and a tank top, but the need to look her best egged her on. When she finally came downstairs, she found him in the kitchen with a beer, reading his phone.

"Anything interesting happen while I was in the shower?"

"Nope. World's still spinning. Lucky for us." He finally peeked up at her. "Lucky for *me*. Geez, you look great."

She smiled and curtsied. "Thank you, sir."

He led her to the back door, and they walked through the patio on their way to the path to the dock.

He led her through the foliage to his boats. No longer a stranger, she stepped onto the small cabin cruiser and immediately went for the life vests. He sighed when she handed his to him.

"I'm not going to fall out and hit my head."

"Humor me."

He put on the life vest, then helped her with hers. The first time he'd secured it, she'd barely noticed the brush of his fingers. Knowing this was a date, every touch, every sweep of his hands against her arms, chest and tummy whispered through her, bringing back the best parts of their time together as teenagers.

When she was settled, he started the boat. In a few minutes, they were docking at a lively, noisy island. They walked down the pier toward the street. Reggae music poured from a tiki bar crowded with people spilling out onto the sidewalk, dressed in everything from ragged cutoff shorts to sparkling dresses and tuxes.

"Could be a wedding party."

They walked past, but she turned to look back, totally curious. "Really a wedding party?"

He shrugged. "Why not?"

"Who can afford this stuff?"

He chuckled. "It's not as expensive as you think." He pointed down the street, toward colorful houses, some with white fences. "A lot of those homes are rentals. It's not much more expensive than renting a house in Ocean City or Virginia Beach."

Her head tilted as she thought about that. "This is like a town of tourists?"

"Yes and no. Some of these houses were passed down from generations of people who were born here. Other houses are second homes. And some houses are second homes that people can afford because they rent them out half the year. So, we have tourists, part-time residents and residents."

"Should be an interesting bunch."

"Oh, they are."

He guided her to a restaurant a block away from the dock. They were led to a table outside and she eagerly looked at the menu. "I'm ordering tuna."

He groaned. "Really? You're trying to make me feel guilty?"

She lowered the menu so she could grin at him. "You've had it all over me the whole time we've been here. Feels good that you slipped up and I can tease you."

"I've had it all over you?" He snorted. "You with your sad eyes that let me know you needed a rest, so I let you stay?" He harrumphed. "And on your terms. *You've* been calling the shots."

One of her eyebrows rose. "Oh, so you haven't wanted to stay out all day fishing."

"Yes, I have wanted to stay out all day fishing."

"So, I didn't call any shots. Which means if anyone's on higher ground it's you."

He sighed dramatically. "Maybe."

"Maybe?"

"All right. I have a few more bucks than you and a few more toys."

She considered that. "I don't think I have *any* toys."

"Not even a sled?"

That made her laugh. "Nope. No sled."

"I refuse to feel guilty for having money."

A soft breeze blew to them. It smelled like the sea, sunblock and happiness. "I wouldn't. If I were you, I'd *live* here."

"There were days I considered it. Trace

spends most of his time in Italy. He jets back and forth for important things. But he goes to a lot of meetings via the internet."

"Really?"

"Yeah. He owns a vineyard with his fiancée. Her dad just bought a second vineyard and they're part of the renovations on that one too. Beautiful places both of them."

"You've been there?"

"Yes. After my first visit I understood why Trace settled there. And not just because Marcia grew up there. There are some spots that call to people. Trace's was Italy." He glanced around. "The Keys are mine."

She looked around too. "I get that."

They were quiet for a minute as they studied the menu. When the waitress came over, they ordered wine. She scurried away to get a bottle, returning with a nice red and a basket of bread, ready to take their orders.

Reese really did choose the tuna. Cade rolled his eyes before ordering shrimp scampi.

"I love shrimp scampi."

He caught her gaze. "We can share."

"Don't think this is getting you part of my tuna."

He laughed, then grew quiet as he took a sip of wine. After a few seconds, he said, "Do you think my dad saw something that we didn't?"

She glanced across the warm bread at him. "Excuse me?"

"My dad. I mean, he clearly set us up. Do you think he saw something about us that we didn't see?"

Fear skittered through her. Not because she thought Martin might tell her secrets. He didn't know them. But even so, Cade was edging them toward a discussion about her. Her life.

Or God forbid, the future.

His note edged into her thoughts. The way he'd sounded like his teenage self. The guy who'd wanted to marry her, have a gaggle of kids and live happily ever after.

She held her voice steady as she said, "Something we didn't see… Like what?"

He shrugged. "I don't know. I'm wondering if he thinks we never got over our first love."

She snorted. "Don't even try to say you've never dated anyone else."

"Actually, I was married."

She didn't know why that surprised her. He was gorgeous and rich. Of course he'd found a woman who wanted to marry him.

Surprise unexpectedly morphed into sadness that he had replaced her when she'd never really replaced him. She'd fallen in love once. She'd actually loved Tony enough to marry him, but his proposal had ended in disaster, not merely heartbreak, a feeling of failure followed by complete worthlessness—

She took a breath to stop that train of thought. So she'd never gotten married? After the breakup with Tony, she hadn't *wanted* to get married. And Cade had. She could accept that in a person who was only a vacation fling.

"I'd say congratulations, but you said you *were* married. I'm guessing it ended."

He winced. "Nasty divorce."

"Like parents, like son?"

"No. We didn't buy guns and throw plates. It was more that after two years of torturing me, pouting over perceived slights, publicly embarrassing me, my ex wanted a share in the original corporation. She wanted half of my one-third when the business had been well established before she entered my life. She had no hand in helping us build it. And we had a prenup that gave her a generous settlement." He shook his head. "But she fought like a woman scorned when she was the one who cheated on me. I had to hire a bulldog for an attorney."

It sounded enough like his parents' divorce that she blinked. Luckily, it wasn't her place to point that out.

He shrugged. "It ended up being a good thing that the marriage failed. In our final outrageous argument that totally ended things, she told me that she didn't want kids." He sighed. "I know I was stressed out at the time, but everything about our marriage came into focus in her rant. I suddenly saw that I'd gotten married because I'd wanted a family. Hearing her say she didn't was like culture shock. But the next day at work I realized Trace and Wyatt were my family. I didn't need to build something I already had. So now, marriage is off the table for me."

She stared at him. In what he probably considered a straightforward statement of facts, he'd addressed at least two important subjects. First, he'd gotten married to have a family. *To have kids.* Second, he didn't want to get married again. His friends had replaced his desire to have a family.

Cautious, she said, "You're sure that reasoning wasn't just the emotion of a bad divorce?"

"I don't make decisions like that lightly."

He might not make decisions lightly, but this was the kind of thing she needed to be 100 percent certain about. "So, you've given up on having kids?"

"I don't think you understand how busy I am. How little time I would have for children." He snorted. "That was Brenda's number one complaint. I had no time for *her.* It cost me a pretty penny to get out of a marriage that had been a judgment error. I subconsciously went in looking for something specific and didn't realize I'd gotten the whole thing wrong until that day she blew up and I saw we'd never been on the same page. I took some time and really thought about what I wanted out of life... And realized I already have it."

Reese's head spun. If all that was true—and she had no reason to doubt it—he had just made their situation perfect. Even if their fling lasted beyond this vacation, there would be no talk of the future, marriage, kids. No horrible sense that they would eventually have an uncomfortable conversation. No waiting for the other shoe to drop when she'd be forced to put all her secrets out on the table.

Satisfied and knowing it was time to change the subject or at least lighten the mood, she glanced out at the blue water. "You think you lost out on your divorce, but you still have enough money to own an island."

He grinned. "Yes."

"So, stop whining."

He laughed, but it wasn't the easy laugh of a guy who was happy. He was nervous, as if there was something else he wanted to tell her. Maybe another warning before he allowed their relationship to get too personal?

Before he could say anything, the waitress arrived with their food.

As she walked away, Cade picked up his spoon and knife. "I didn't bring up my dad or my divorce to make either of us uncomfortable. My dad throwing us together could have just as easily turned out badly. I should call him and tell him to butt out."

As if Martin would listen. "You could."

Cade sighed. "I shouldn't have to. He knows I'll never get married again. I have the example of his and my mother's glorious marriage, then my own dismal failure." He rolled his eyes. "I'd have to be crazy not to have learned that lesson."

She cautiously said, "Crazy does run in your family." But another thought struck her. He didn't have something else to tell her. He'd brought the discussion back to marriage because she hadn't yet acknowledged or accepted that he didn't want one.

He was a billionaire with money and his sanity to protect. And so far, she'd evaded all his questions and had given him vague replies when he'd talked about himself, about what he wanted and didn't want in his life.

He needed to hear her say she accepted his terms.

"Cade, you didn't have to explain why

you'll never get married. I get it. I'll never marry, either."

He frowned when he looked at her. "Bad divorce?"

"No. I never married." She shrugged. *Her* heartbreak over Tony had taught her the same lesson he'd learned. Marriage wasn't for everyone. "I think I'm not the marrying kind."

He gaped at her. "Really? *You're* not the marrying kind?"

"Don't sound so surprised. I own a business. I want to be successful—"

"You should do the franchise thing I was telling you about."

She blew her breath out on a sigh. "No. Whatever I do, I want to do it my way. And marriage doesn't factor into any of that for me."

"So, we're on the same page?"

She couldn't tell if he intended for that question to sound like they were negotiating an agreement, but her chest and stomach didn't know if they should fall or fill with tingles. Whether he'd intended it or not, he'd opened the door for them to—

Well, do just about anything they wanted. No strings attached. No commitment.

The strangest feeling enveloped her. Part fear, part awe, it rolled through her as anticipation.

Without being bossy or intrusive, he'd proved they really could have a fling and walk away because neither one of them had any illusions about what they were getting into. Just as a smart businessman didn't go into a deal without all the facts, he'd gotten their expectations out on the table.

Her heart jolted. Her breath stuttered.

They were about to go back to his very private island where there was no one to stop them and no one to see if things turned romantic.

CHAPTER EIGHT

AFTER DINNER, THEY STROLLED around the island, getting ice cream, even though both were still full. She talked about her business. He talked about his friends, about Wyatt being handed a baby he didn't even know he had when an old girlfriend popped into his penthouse announcing she was going to United Arab Emirates for her job and he'd have to care for their child.

The more Cade talked, the more she understood his stance on marriage. Only his friend Trace was happily engaged, but he'd had to make huge concessions in how he worked. Part of the reason the Three Musketeers—that's what Reese had decided to call them—were so successful was the fluidity of their lives.

She understood that because her virtually nonexistent personal life was part of why she was able to create and manage her own business. She filled in for workers who called off. She could do her billing and banking in the middle of the night. She could sit on her sofa, watching television, and create schedules, read résumés, study situation reports.

All her time was hers.

Just as all of Cade's time belonged to him.

They returned late enough that the lights on the path blinked on, and they strolled up the walkway to the patio holding hands. Clearly happy from their date, he smiled down at her.

"I'm going to take a midnight swim. Wanna join me?"

Anticipation stole through her again. She knew exactly what he was asking. But as limited as their remaining time was, she decided to take the night and let everything about them settle in. Not merely in her brain, but in his too.

Plus, the evening had been perfect and if she'd misinterpreted his intentions when he'd explained that he'd never remarry, she did not want to ruin it. She wanted to take home the wonderful memory of good food and wine, and conversations that spoke of connection and easy happiness.

She rose to her tiptoes and brushed her lips across his mouth. "Thanks, but I'm actually very tired. I think I'll go to my room."

He caught her elbows as she pulled away and brought her back to him for a proper kiss. His lips swiped over hers, then nipped until she opened her mouth and allowed their tongues to twine.

Arousal built. Soft and sweet at first, then hot and greedy. But she stood by her decision to give them one more day to make sure this was really what they both wanted.

She pulled back and pressed her palm to his cheek. If she were being honest, she had to admit there were times when this felt like a dream. Too good to be true. And maybe that's why she sought the confirmation of another day.

"Good night."

He held her gaze, his blue eyes gleaming, his breathing shallow. "Good night."

She turned and walked into the house, remembering their first kiss all those years ago, the way he'd grinned as he ambled down the sidewalk of her parents' home, and she let her lips lift into a goofy smile. She totally understood why he'd grinned. There was nothing like the feeling that you'd found someone who understood you and someone you understood. And she wanted to hug that to herself for another few hours.

Just in case the bubble burst.

She could have thought herself a pessimist. But life had not been kind to her. The rape had been bad enough. Six years later, the discovery that she couldn't have kids had cost her a man she'd loved.

But with Cade not wanting a commitment or a family, there'd be no talk of marriage. No reason to discuss the issue that had caused Tony to look at her with pity and walk away. No reason to even believe their relationship would be longer than their stay here.

It really was perfect.

For something designed to be temporary.

Cade woke early the next morning and raced downstairs. He made scrambled eggs, toast and bacon. By the time the scent woke Reese and brought her to him, sniffing the air as she entered the kitchen, he was pouring champagne into orange juice in fancy flutes.

"What's all this?"

In her tiny tank top and pajama pants, with her pink cheeks and disheveled hair, she looked warm and sleepy. He imagined if he touched her now, she'd melt into him and he could kiss her senseless in about ten seconds.

"There's no point in having money if you don't enjoy it."

She chuckled. "I'm not much of a break-fast eater."

He gestured to the food on the center island. "You're going to turn all this down?"

She picked up a piece of bacon and nibbled. "Oh, Lord, that's good."

"Haven't had bacon in a while, have you?"

She took another bite of the bacon, closing her eyes in ecstasy, making him laugh.

"Grab the mimosas. I'll put everything else on a tray and follow you out to the patio."

She happily agreed. When she opened the door and saw the table, set with good china and a centerpiece of fresh flowers, she stopped. "What time did you get up this morning?"

He headed for the table. "Six." He winced. "Maybe five thirty."

Her head tilted as she examined the display. Then she took a breath, gazing out at the blue water, before she turned to him. "This is perfect. Thank you."

Her appreciation of simple things had always moved him. When it came to material goods, he had everything he wanted. Her blue-collar family provided necessities and only a few extras. She'd never complained—was always happy with what she had. But when he'd done anything nice for her, she'd blossomed. And his heart had bubbled with joy.

As it did right now.

He had to swallow before he could say, "You're welcome."

He set the tray of food on the table, then pulled out her chair for her.

She ate more than he did because he found himself watching her instead of eating. He couldn't remember ever being so happy, so content. Realizing they had only today, Thursday and Friday, he vowed to make every one of those days the best he could for them both. He worked hard. She worked hard. Their private lives were scant at best. Fate had given them some time together and he intended to take advantage of that.

Even if it didn't result in them sleeping together.

She'd run away from the perfect opportunity the night before. Probably because she'd wanted to make sure it was the right thing for them. If that was the case, he'd keep them going in that direction.

If she'd run because she didn't want what he did, then he'd be a gentleman. A good host. Because he liked her.

Not entirely sure which way she was thinking, he kept all his options open.

"I thought we'd fish this morning."

She peered over at him. "We?"

"Aren't you curious?"

She set down her bacon, tucked her hair behind her ear and asked, "About what?"

"If nothing else, you should wonder how someone could spend eight hours alone on a boat."

"Yeah, that does sort of make me ponder your sanity."

He laughed. "We leave in ten minutes. I'll text Nina to come and put all this away and we can head out to the boat."

She frowned, clearly not totally on board with the idea. "What should I wear?"

"I liked that little pink bikini you had on when I got here."

Her frown deepened, wrinkling her brow. "I don't need special fishing clothes?"

"You can wear a life vest if it makes it more official for you."

She rose from the table. "The life vest is essential equipment." She turned toward the house, then faced him again. "You're wearing one too, bucko."

She pivoted toward the house and he laughed so easily and so naturally, his thoughts jumbled. He'd never felt this way with any other woman and for a flash he wondered if that didn't mean something. He couldn't imagine growing tired of her. He couldn't imagine her getting demanding. He could see them having discussions, making decisions together—

Then his phone vibrated, and he saw the

caller was his dad and those thoughts evaporated into stardust, along with unicorns and other things that didn't actually exist.

With memories of his dad's stroke still fluttering through him, he didn't bother with hello, just said, "Everything okay?"

"Yeah. Yeah. It's all good here."

"Go out with your nurse?"

His father had the good graces to laugh. "Funny thing about that. I only told you I was interested in her to get you to go to the island with Reese, but weird things started happening. She really is as wonderful as I'd said. And she's pretty. And nice."

"Well, well, well... Maybe you are changing."

"So, I'm guessing your good mood means you aren't mad at me?"

Cade blew his breath out on a long sigh. "The first time in twelve years that I come home and you meddle?"

"But you're happy."

"We're getting along."

"You're more than getting along. Your voice is light and springy..."

"Where do you come up with stuff like *light and springy*? I don't even know what a springy voice is."

His dad laughed. "I'm just saying that maybe

if you'd come home sooner, I could have gotten you and Reese back together sooner."

His blood turned to ice water. The thought of "being together" with anyone brought up all his defenses. Worse, his dad *had* expected something permanent to happen. Something neither he nor Reese wanted. He knew that because of their conversation the night before, but he didn't know much else. He'd given her at least three good ins to tell him about her life, and she'd rejected them all.

Could be a warning sign that something in her life could screw up their simple tryst. Or it could be that Ohio was as boring as he remembered. A couple of hours on the boat would probably have her warming up to him enough that she'd start talking and hopefully she'd confirm why she'd raced away the night before.

That was the plan, and he wasn't deviating from it because his dad had called and messed with his thinking.

"We're not back together. We're getting along because we both needed a rest. And this could have blown up in your face if Reese and I weren't mature adults."

"Actually, that's my point, Cade. You are mature adults now. Things could be totally different this time... Oh, I gotta go. Yolanda's here."

With that he disconnected the call and Cade sat staring at the phone. He hadn't had the chance to say his piece about meddling, and, worse, he'd given his dad the wrong idea. Then his dad had hung up before Cade could change it. Whether he'd been forced to disconnect the call or not, it was clear his dad was playing matchmaker for two people who didn't want to be matched. He'd tried finding a mate and failed miserably. And Reese had said she wasn't the marrying kind. She wasn't looking for a commitment—though she'd never satisfactorily explained why—

The horrible sense that she was hiding something filled him again, but he shook his head to clear it. It was probably nothing but the aftereffects of feeling manipulated after talking to his dad.

Reese came out of the house in a filmy white cover-up that showed peeks of pink gingham. *She'd worn the bikini he liked.*

He could jump the gun and think that was proof that she liked him and hadn't left him alone on the patio the night before because she didn't want anything to happen between them. But they had a whole morning on the boat to figure this out and he needed to get it right. Not make assumptions.

"Are you going fishing in your shorts?"

"I could. But I want to change." He displayed his phone. "My dad called."

She winced. "Did you yell at him?"

"I'm not secure enough in his recovery that I'd yell at a guy who just had a stroke."

She snorted a laugh and walked to the table, where she chugged the rest of her mimosa. "Go get dressed. The sooner we get out on the water, the sooner we get home."

He said, "Okay," and headed into the house. But he stopped in the kitchen as the strangest thought hit him. What if she wanted to get back from fishing because she had...plans for them?

His heart stuttered at the thought that she might try to seduce him, and he snickered at his foolishness. He needed to get a hold of his wayward imagination and let anything between them unfold one step at a time. With clear understanding at every step.

His libido protested that that was assuming a lot, and he should make a move. He told his libido to settle down and be patient. She'd told him she still found him attractive in their kiss the night before. The other stuff might take a little longer to sort through. He could not get this wrong, the way he had with Brenda.

They drove the fishing boat out onto the clear blue water. He reached into the cooler for a beer and offered her one.

She sniffed. "After a mimosa, a beer would be an insult to my palate."

He laughed. He'd stopped the boat in a spot so far out that the shore was like a thin line on the horizon. He showed her the rods, the bait.

"So, you have special bait that's designed to lure the fish in?"

"Thus, the word *lure*. It's a fishing *lure*."

She frowned. "That hardly seems fair."

"Why are you taking the side of the fish when we're attempting to catch dinner?"

"I just think it should be an even match."

He shrugged. "They have advantages. We have advantages. Trust me, it's a fair fight."

"We'll see."

He stood on the stern, wearing a life vest, not having a second beer, wondering about the fairness of his lure for the first time ever—because she was bossy. But it felt right, like a check-and-balance system that made him laugh and gave him the sense that she wasn't just a visitor. She was a part of this fishing trip.

He grabbed his favorite rod, remembering how he and Reese had clicked all those years ago. When they'd talked about marriage and kids it had seemed right. Like an inevitability. They'd automatically assumed a good life, a stable, happy life, meant getting married and having kids—

Probably because her family was so normal and the one thing he'd always wanted was to be normal.

Now he knew he didn't need those things. He already was normal. A normal businessman. He didn't need anything else.

Too bad he hadn't figured all that out before he'd married Brenda.

He faced Reese again. "Okay. So now that we have the bait—"

"Lure—your unfair advantage—"

He sighed. "Now that the *lure* is on the hook, I'm going to cast off. Like this." He pulled the rod back over his shoulder and swung it around. The reel spun, sending yards and yards of line into the air until it landed far away from the boat.

"Wow. How are you going to know when you have a fish?"

"The line will jerk and go taut."

"Ah."

He held the rod as she stared at the line. A minute turned into two, which became three and then somehow seven.

"Is it supposed to take this long?"

"There's no time limit on how long it takes for fish to see the bait." He reeled the line in and cast it out again, keeping the lure moving.

"If there are no fish here, we'll move to another spot, hoping to find them."

She smiled out at the sea. "Makes sense."

Her serene face made him glad he'd brought her with him that morning. She loved being out on the water. He did too. He loved to fish but he also knew part of the allure was being far away from everyone and everything, on water that caught sunlight and reflected it so well that the whole world seemed to sparkle.

She removed her cover-up and stretched out.

Everything male inside him awakened at the sight of all the supple flesh exposed by her skimpy bikini. In the years that had passed, her breasts had grown while it seemed her waist had tightened. He'd bet he could span it with his hands—

Realizing he needed a cold shower or at the very least a splash in the face, he said, "You know, if you want, we could stop fishing and swim."

She opened one eye. "No need. I think I might catch a nap."

He reeled his line in and cast it out again. "And you also refuse to swim with fish."

"There is that."

He laughed. "You're funny. Different. But the same."

Without opening her eyes, she said, "You already pointed out that I turned into a coward. I say *mature adult*. But, hey, you have a right to your opinion."

His rod tensed and he looked out over the water, staring at his line. Nothing more happened so he relaxed but by that time he glanced at her again, he saw she was asleep. He could have stood and stared at her all day but forced himself back to casting his line.

As odd as it sounded, realizing he had created a normal life for himself began to erase the worry that Reese might have a secret. His very good, very normal life was in Manhattan. Even if she had a secret, anything that happened between them would be confined to this trip. Plus, she'd said the important things. That she wasn't interested in a permanent relationship. Whatever they had probably wouldn't last beyond this week.

He could stop wondering. In the end, any secret she had didn't matter. They weren't trying to re-create the idyllic life they'd imagined as teens. They were two ships passing in the night.

Eventually, he caught two tuna and drank another beer. Warm air and silence enveloped them in their own little world. He loved being in the stillness of the ocean, but he loved even more that he and Reese were reconciling their past. Not by creating a future. But by behaving like adults.

He caught a third fish, then put away his rod and prepared to head home.

"Hey, sleepyhead. You have to get up. You're going to have a suntan in the shape of a life vest."

She yawned and stretched, and he didn't stay around to watch the way her muscles would pull beneath soft, sun-warmed skin. He didn't want to see her hair shining or her green eyes twinkle with happiness. He already wanted to make love to her so badly he couldn't focus on anything else. No sense making things worse until he knew she wanted what he did. He needed to be certain she hadn't bolted the night before because she didn't want to become lovers. That she'd stopped them only to be sure that was what they both wanted.

The trip on the boat was supposed to get her talking or at least help him see if she agreed that their fun together should go further—

Actually, it might have. A woman who didn't get the concept of fishing, who didn't want to swim with fish, who didn't drink beer...had spent three hours on a boat with him.

If he asked himself why, the only answer

could be that she liked spending time with him.
Or maybe just plain liked *him*.

Enough to want to make love?

He guessed he was about to find out.

CHAPTER NINE

WHEN THEY RETURNED to the house, Cade was different. The second they arrived on the patio, he tossed his shirt and jumped into the infinity pool. As a person who lived in Ohio, the heat got to Reese too, and she shucked her cover up and joined him.

Doing a slow backstroke, she floated on top of the water.

From beside her, Cade said, "This is nice."

She opened one eye. "Yeah." The perfection of it overwhelmed her and she pushed herself upright to tread water. "Seriously, thank you for letting me stay."

He laughed. "It's been fun having you here."

She smiled.

He smiled.

For a few seconds they simply started at each other. Maybe remembering the past. Maybe enjoying the moment. Maybe realizing their intense connection was as natural as the rhythm of each heartbeat.

Maybe deciding that was okay.

Everything was okay here on the island.

A force that felt a lot like gravity pulled them together. Their lips met slowly, easily as they floated in the warm, soothing water. He slid one hand around her neck and the other to her lower back to steady her, but she eased her legs up, hooking them around his waist. He took advantage and moved his second hand to her back so he could tilt her and deepen the kiss.

The feeling of déjà vu enveloped her. All fear flitted away and was replaced by a sense of security so strong it was as if someone pressed a button and tossed her back in time.

This was how she'd felt making love before she was raped. The sensations that slid through her were like coming home. Like being herself again.

Finally.

The word echoed through her and a desire to weep nearly overtook her, so she reached around to unsnap the top of her bikini and then threw it to a convenient chaise. Her breasts met his chest, her nipples hardening on contact. Her soul filled with contentment that knitted to reality. This was how it was supposed to be. Not frantic to stay one step ahead of the memory of fear. Not simple and regimented, as it had been with Tony. But fun and joyful. Natural like breathing. But passionate. So intense that thought wasn't necessary.

And that's what she needed. The reminder that every time a man touched her, she didn't need to explain to herself why this feeling was allowed, why it was different from Finn.

She could simply enjoy.

The kiss went on and on. His hands roamed her back. Contentment rippled through her like the warm water bumping her legs and butt. Arousal awoke in her belly.

He broke the kiss to nuzzle her neck. "You're so beautiful."

She laughed. "So you've said."

"Because it's true."

She skimmed her hands down his back, enjoying the solid muscles before she ran her tongue along his shoulders to his chest. "You're salty."

"The curse of being a fisherman."

She laughed again and he brought her back to him for another long, lingering kiss. This time his hands moved from her back to her breasts and belly. She answered his movements but took them one step further, allowing her fingers to slide beneath the elastic of his swimming trunks. She pushed them down enough that eventually he kicked out of them. Then he slipped his hands into her bikini bottoms and had them off and tossed to the chaise in what seemed like two seconds.

Naked, aroused, they slid against each other in the warm water. Her heart filled with happiness and her skin prickled with goose bumps when he lowered his head and took a straining nipple into his mouth. Her hands cruised his torso, sliding farther and farther down, eventually stalling on the muscles of his butt.

His lips roved her chest. Her muscles trembled with a longing so fierce it demanded to be satisfied. Without giving him any indication of what she was about to do, she shifted in the smooth water and joined them.

His head fell back, and he groaned. She buried her face in his neck. Their connection had always been electric. This was beyond compare.

It took only a few seconds before they found a simple, easy rhythm that built into a frenzy of need. Every cell in her body came alive. He kissed each inch of her skin that he could reach. Her bones dissolved into molten lava. Need and greed bubbled through her, a desire to take, not wait. It seemed she'd waited forever.

But as an orgasm stole her breath and everything inside her melted with joy, he sucked in a long drink of air and said, "Refresh my memory... Why'd we break up again?"

She laughed because she knew that's what he expected of her. But the question in his voice sounded real, sounded like it was coming from a guy who'd never reconciled their ending.

And in a way she hadn't either. It had been too abrupt. Other things had consumed her energy—while school consumed his. They'd made mistakes and been drawn away from each other by circumstances. And both still had a bit of a hole in their hearts.

Maybe that was why fate had brought them together for this week?

They needed to talk about that night.

They drifted on the water for a few seconds before he leaned down and nibbled her neck. Sated, happy, it took a minute before he could bring himself back to reality.

"No one's ever pushed me to the point that I've had unprotected sex."

Laughing, she ran her hands down his back. "Not to worry. I never have unprotected sex. We're safe."

"What about pregnancy?"

She stiffened. "No worry about that."

He lifted his head to catch her gaze. "Are you sure?"

"Yeah."

Something in her voice wasn't quite right. "Are you okay?"

"Seriously? I just had some of the best sex of my life. Of course I'm not okay. I'm…sort of wonderful."

He anchored himself against the pool wall, then reached out, caught her hand and tugged her beside him. "I'm sort of wonderful too."

A weak, confusing laugh escaped her. He peered down at her again. "You seem to be losing your wonderful."

She winced. "I think there are some things we need to talk about."

The secret.

The thing he'd sensed she'd been hiding.

He wasn't sure he wanted to hear that now. He'd sorted his past and their nonexistent future. There was no need.

He tilted his head as he studied her. "All week I tried to get you to tell me about your life and you pick now? I was going to wait twelve to fifteen minutes and show you how crazy I am about you again."

She trailed her fingers up his chest. "I was hoping you'd say that." She peeked up at him.

"But if I don't tell you some of this now, I'll never tell you."

Fear stuttered through him. He'd let her stay in the hope that eventually she'd explain why she'd broken up with him. What if that was the thing she'd been keeping from him? Her secret.

"When you first left for Harvard, I went to a football game with my friend Janie."

He held her gaze, not sure he wanted to hear this now—not when they were so happy. Not when he wanted to keep everything simple between them. So many years had passed. They seemed to have forgiven each other. Fear that she'd ruin the few days they had left stiffened his muscles, made his chest ache.

She hesitated, her tongue darting out to moisten her lips. "Right before the game ended, when everybody was whipped into a frenzy because the score was tied, Finn Mc-Cully kind of half dragged, half begged me to come under the bleachers with him."

"Finn McCully?" The name jarred him out of his depressing thoughts. "I haven't heard his name in forever."

"There's a reason for that." She sucked in a breath. "He offered me beer and I refused. He gave me a hard time, insisting that he knew I drank—which I didn't—and I was being a snob not partying with him."

Not at all expecting that, Cade gaped at her. "What the hell was he talking about?"

"I don't know. It was so out of character that I just got myself away from him. Janie and I walked home and after she veered off onto her driveway, I got the horrible feeling I was being followed."

"I do not like where this is going."

"Well, you're going to hate the rest because he pulled me down an alley between two houses into the garage Dusty Buchanan used to do off-the-books bodywork on cars."

Cade's heart stopped. The air he drew in felt like wet cement. Finn McCully had been a big guy. Not fat. Tall and muscled. Cade couldn't see little sixteen-year-old Reese being any match for him.

His chest tightened with an emotion that somehow combined sympathy and fury.

"He told me that I thought I was so special. A princess. Because I was dating you. Then he raped me."

Cade's breath hissed out. "Son of a bitch."

"I don't even think he realized that what he was doing was wrong. He was drunk and so smug and proud of himself as if he should win an award. Then he let me go without argument. I raced home. My parents called the police and took me to the hospital. There was a rape kit, and he was arrested."

A weird sense of total disbelief rippled through him. She wasn't a liar, but his parents lived in that small town. It was farfetched at best that he wouldn't have heard this story.

"How do I not know any of this?"

"Because there was a plea deal. My parents worried about me, about gossip, and backlash, and the DA offered Finn a reasonable punishment, so we agreed. The thing of it was Finn wasn't sixteen. He was still a minor. He got some jail time and probation and had to register as a sex offender."

"That's it?"

"His parents also moved out of town."

He remembered that. Vaguely. Which was why Cade barely remembered him, why he hadn't even heard Finn's name in forever.

"They promised to get him help and keep him away from me. Which was what my parents believed I needed. Finn's dad also said they wanted to be closer to the detention facility where he would be serving his sentence. Finn had to agree to therapy and Alcoholics Anonymous... Because believe it or not, he didn't remember any of it. Said he blacked out." She pulled in a breath. "But DNA doesn't lie."

Cade gasped. "He didn't use a condom?"

She hesitated. "No."

He shifted away from the pool wall so he could stand in front of her, look at her face as she spoke. Sorrow for her hit him like a punch in the gut, along with a red-hot anger that knew no bounds. "I could kill him."

She looked up at him. "Really? I'm not quite at the let-bygones-be-bygones stage, but I won't let him steal the rest of my life. He took a million things from me, Cade. Like our relationship. And other things. Little things. Big things. Things I can't even define or describe. I won't let him have anything else."

That made so much sense, his anger lessened. He rubbed his hand along the back of his neck. "Why didn't you tell me?" Upset for her, he looked at the sky, then back at her again. "You should have told me. All these years I thought you dumped me because you'd found somebody else."

"I did try to tell you." She took a breath. "I called and called that night after I got back from the hospital."

He frowned at her.

"I left messages, but you didn't return my call for four days." She closed her eyes. "By then I'd lost my nerve."

"You should have found a way to tell me—"

"After it took you four days to return six

calls? There was *nothing* you could have done. My parents made sure he was brought to justice. I went to therapy. Dealt with it all." She caught his gaze. "I'm okay."

Confusion and sympathy coiled through him. His voice soft, he asked, "Are you? Really?"

She shook her head and swam to the pool ladder. "You know what? I think I'll go back inside for a while."

She was out of the water and swiping her bathing suit and cover-up off the chaise lounge before he even realized what was happening.

Disappointed with himself for being so clumsy, for undoubtedly saying all the wrong things, for not giving her comfort and unconditional support, he sprang out of the water to follow her.

But he stopped by his swimming trunks, putting them on to give himself a few minutes to think.

Part of him wanted to follow her to her room. The other part knew he was out of his depth. His parents throwing plates at each other was nothing compared to a sixteen-year-old girl being violated by a smug drunk. He wanted to hold her, to somehow make everything okay, to protect her from anything ever happening to her again… But when he had turned sympathetic, she'd run.

She hadn't run when he'd asked questions. She hadn't backed down when his voice might have sounded skeptical.

She'd run when he'd wanted to hold her. To sympathize. To be angry on her behalf.

He rubbed his hand across his mouth. *Oh, Lord, was he out of his element.*

But he did understand one thing. She didn't want him to feel sorry for her. His Reese had never wanted pity or sympathy or for anyone to underestimate her.

Which meant she wanted to be treated normally.

After twelve years that made perfect sense. Undoubtedly, she *had* dealt with it. She'd made a good life for herself. She might not be exactly the person she'd told him she wanted to be when she grew up, but she was close.

The truth of that settled into him slowly. After he'd told her about Roger Burkey, he'd appreciated that she hadn't pushed him for more information or smothered him. Telling her the truth of what was bothering him had bonded them enough that when he'd caught her hand to lead her to the patio, he hadn't wanted to let go. He'd kissed her.

Sharing his story had brought them closer. That's why they'd been so easygoing with each other on the boat, in the pool. And why she'd told him about Finn McCully. He'd trusted her with his troubles. Then she'd trusted him with a secret.

It was another step.

And he had blown it.

Sitting on the balcony off her suite, Reese saw Cade walk up from the dock. He had three fish on a string—fish he'd obviously forgotten when they'd left the boat. He took them around to the side of the house, where she couldn't see him.

She leaned back in her chair and would have fallen asleep but she couldn't tolerate just sitting around, upset that he'd ruined her confession before she could finish, before she could assure him that she was fine. Adjusted. Normal in all the ways that mattered.

His sympathy dragged her right back to those weeks, when her whole life had changed, and she was barely old enough to deal with it. She wanted to shake him silly because she wasn't that girl anymore.

But wasn't that the point?

She wasn't that girl anymore and neither was she the girl Cade had fallen in love with.

Not about to sit around and brood about something she'd long ago survived, she bounced up in her seat, slipped into shoes and retrieved a bike from the garage.

She rode around the island, letting her anxiety and borderline anger with Cade dissolve into nothing in the fresh island air. By the time she returned, the scent of grilling fish filled the area. Stowing her bike in the garage, she decided to pretend nothing had happened and walked through the house, directly to the patio.

"Hey! What smells good?"

"Dinner."

She glanced at the table that had been set for two. Wine in an ice bucket. Pretty glasses. Dishes she would call good china.

"What's all this?"

"I didn't want to put tuna and veggies grilled to perfection on paper plates."

She laughed, but inside she died a little. He'd made a gorgeous dinner, set the table and would probably treat her with kid gloves for the rest of the trip. No more fun. No more laughing. Just him fawning over her as if she were a fragile doll. Not a woman who'd struggled and persevered.

She couldn't imagine what he'd do if she told him she couldn't have kids and thanked her lucky stars that he'd turned that into a nonissue.

Swallowing her disappointment, she said, "Is there anything I can do to help?"

"Yeah. Check the fridge to see if there's potato salad."

She shook her head. "You're a creature of habit."

"Which probably makes it very easy for my shopper to keep the place stocked and me happy."

Turning to the open patio doors, she said, "Probably."

She found the potato salad and would have brought it straight out, except he'd gone to such trouble to make the table pretty that she thought she might as well join in on the fake happiness. Disappointment returned in a wave. His reaction proved they'd never really get back to the place they'd been when they were kids. Despite everything she'd felt while they were making love, they'd never hit that level of trust where they could tell each other everything and accept each other for who they were.

And that was her real dream. The thing she wanted more than anything else. That she could be honest with someone, be herself with someone, and they'd still love her.

When she reached the outdoor table and set the glass bowl in the center, he glanced at it, then at her.

"What's that?"

"A nice dish to match the other things."

He frowned. "Really?"

"Yes."

"I only brought out the good dishes because of the tuna."

She looked at him.

He lifted one of the tuna steaks. "Tell me that isn't beautiful."

She laughed uneasily. From watching him fish, she knew he thought of being out on his boat as only one step below religion. Maybe he really did think the fish was worth good plates? "It's beautiful."

"Okay, then."

She took a breath. He sort of *was* behaving like himself. She could stew about his reaction to her confession and ruin their last days together or she could face it outright. Since she was an outright sort of girl, she knew they had to have the conversation.

"All right. Thank you. I do love the tuna. But I just want to make sure you don't feel sorry for me. That you treat me normally."

He put the tuna back on the grill and walked over to her. "I can't treat you normally."

Sadness permeated her soul. "At least you're honest."

"I can't treat you normally because I believe

you deserve to be treated special. When a guy really likes a girl, he wants to treat her special. Not because of her life circumstances but because it's what guys do. I'm guessing it dates back to the cavemen, when a guy would go out and kill a bear so his woman would have fur to keep her warm at night."

She stared at him as her face scrunched with confusion. "What?"

"Caveman. Deep down I think all men have a little caveman in them and if they don't, maybe they should."

Now she really wasn't following him.

He put his hands on her shoulders. "I like you. I like you so much that sometimes I can't breathe for the happiness that bubbles up when I realize you really are here with me. I want to do nice things for you. That's all. No deeper meaning than that. We have a couple of days. I want to enjoy them. I didn't mean to insult you. It was all a shock for me. But I'm over that. And I vote we take advantage of the rest of our time."

In total agreement, she rose to her tiptoes and brushed a kiss across his lips. "Okay."

He smiled. "Okay."

She truly hoped he meant that.

CHAPTER TEN

THEIR DINNER WAS FABULOUS. Reese told him it was the best food she'd eaten in forever. He would have thought she was overcompensating, working to make him believe her trauma was no big deal. But he remembered what he'd concluded about how he had to trust that she really was fine and treat her the way he had been.

So they teased and laughed, cuddling together on a chaise to watch a movie on a big-screen TV that rose from the stone counter a few feet down from the grill.

She gaped at him. "You have everything."

He looked down at her. "I do now."

She huffed out a dramatic sigh. "Don't say things like that. You don't want anything permanent. I don't want anything permanent. We're just supposed to be silly."

Worry seeped into his soul.

They hadn't only been silly. Surely it meant

something that they'd told each other some of the worst events of their lives?

He immediately convinced himself their confidences might have been nothing more than catching each other up on the years that had passed. He'd already decided this was a moment snatched out of time for reconnecting and fun. It was Wednesday night. Only Thursday and Friday left. Then this was over. She'd be gone. He'd return to Manhattan. His real life. The little piece of normalcy he'd carved for himself.

Their being together was a fluke. A respite. He wouldn't ruin it.

He didn't let himself think any further than that as they watched the movie. When it ended and another movie began, he slid lower on the chaise, pulling her with him. He nuzzled closer. She did too. Her hands drifted to his shoulders as his found her waist. Peace and contentment were overshadowed by common sense.

"We can't do what I want to do on a chaise lounge."

"We used to."

"We were younger and more agile." He nuzzled her neck. "Besides, I'd like to have you in my bed."

She cuddled closer. "So romantic."

He laughed, rose from the chaise and caught

her hand to help her stand. Without a word, he led her through the kitchen up two flights of stairs and to the master bedroom. When he opened the door on the room with sharp red-and-black geometric designs and a white shag carpet between the bed and the door to the master bath, she gasped.

"Fancy."

He leaned against the doorjamb. "I like to think of it as sexy."

She walked over and slid her hands up his chest. "It is. All bright and bold."

He kissed her. When the kiss ended, she pulled back and smiled.

He studied her face, saw the courage mixed with femininity and remembered why he'd loved her so much. She really was the adult version of the sassy sixteen-year-old he'd loved.

He kissed her again. And again. Eventually they made their way to the bed, where they stripped away each other's clothes and made love like two people so happy to be together there was only one way to express it.

He wondered for a second what would have happened if she hadn't broken up with him, but he couldn't see a happily-ever-after. Had he been told about her rape, he might have killed Finn and he, not Finn, would have been the one to go to jail.

In a roundabout way, his not returning her call might have saved them.

Even though it tore them apart.

But she didn't want to discuss that and neither did he. With no future for them, there was no point in digging too deeply into the past.

He woke the next morning with her exactly where he wanted her. Tucked beneath his arm, nestled against his chest. He took a long breath, running his hands from her shoulders to her butt and back up again with a satisfied, "Mmm..."

Before he could check to see if she was awake, the sensor on the wall alerted him that the front door had been opened. Confused about who might be entering, he slid away from Reese as carefully as he could, threw on a pair of shorts and a T-shirt, in case it was Nina who had let herself in—or God forbid his dad—and headed to the stairway.

At the bottom stood Wyatt, his baby girl Darcy strapped to his chest in the tactical baby carrier that made him look like a Navy SEAL who couldn't find a sitter. Though his beard had been trimmed, his dark hair poked out in all directions.

Cade scrambled down the stairs. "What are you doing here?"

Wyatt made a shh-ing noise, pointing to the

baby who was fast asleep. He whispered, "We needed a little away time."

"I have a friend here!"

Wyatt stopped, studied him. "I know. The woman you showed us in the video call."

"Yes! I told you, she's an old *girlfriend*."

Wyatt grinned. "Well. Well. Well. That's interesting. I'm guessing either you're hoping something will happen between you or something already has." Familiar with the house, he walked toward the kitchen. "I would say I'll leave but you're so secretive about your women that I'm curious."

Cade raced after him. "Leave anyway!"

Wyatt stopped beside the center island. "At least let me see what she looks like."

"You saw her in the phone."

Wyatt rolled his eyes. "Please. I saw a blurry image walking across your kitchen. Let me meet her for real, then I promise I'll call Dennis."

Reese walked into the kitchen. "Call Dennis about what?"

"Our host is having a hissy fit because I brought my baby here for two days of R&R." Wyatt shifted the discussion like a professional.

Reese walked over and peeked at Darcy, then smiled up at Wyatt. "She's adorable!"

"Her mother is gorgeous."

At the mention of Wyatt's ex, Reese glanced around.

"Don't look for her. She's in United Arab Emirates. Which is why I have custody of Darcy. And we wanted two days away. But I don't think Cade's going to let us stay."

"Don't be silly," Reese said easily. "I'll happily leave so you can have some time here."

Cade glared at Wyatt.

"No need for you to leave," Wyatt said smoothly. "In fact, I was thinking exactly the opposite. Darcy and I will spend today and tomorrow, then leave and you guys can add two days onto your time here to make up for the fact that we barged in."

Reese's eyes widened. "I can't add two days—"

Cade crossed his arms, leaning against the kitchen counter, so angry with his meddling partner he could have spit fire.

"Why not? Do you have airline reservations?"

"Sort of. I have a return trip ticket but it's open-ended."

"Meaning, you can pick the time you leave?"

Finally seeing what Wyatt was doing, Cade pressed his lips together. Their "idea man" always had an angle.

"Yes."

"So, instead of going home on Saturday, go

home on Monday. Or Tuesday morning. What-ever. Your choice."

Reese only looked at Wyatt.

Cade laughed and took pity on her. Pushing himself away from the counter, he said, "This isn't a fair debate. Reese hasn't had coffee yet."

"That's right," Wyatt agreed. "She's not awake until she has coffee. Saw that the other morning when Trace and I called."

Reese reached for a coffee pod and hit the start button on the coffee maker. While it warmed up, she retrieved a mug, put in the pod and set the works in motion.

"I don't have a problem with staying an extra two days," Cade interjected casually. "We could go into town again on Sunday. See if we can find a farmers' market."

It was, without a doubt, the stupidest idea he'd ever come up with, but he wasn't as skilled as Wyatt at rearranging the truth to get his own way.

Still, Reese's eyes narrowed as she consid-ered it.

Wyatt didn't wait for a reply. "Thanks. We just want two days. A little time to relax after striking out with nanny interviews all week. Which bedroom is free? I want to put Darcy in her swimsuit."

"I'm in the master. Reese is in the room at the top of the stairs."

As Reese turned to pour cream in her coffee, Wyatt's eyes widened, and he nudged his head in her direction as if totally perplexed by the sleeping arrangements.

Cade stifled a groan. Pushy, meddling Wyatt was going to say something wrong. He just knew it. "Go take care of Darcy. I'll make breakfast."

Wyatt's eyebrows rose. "Those eggs I like?"

"Yes."

"Okay. Cool. See you in ten."

When he was gone, Cade walked to Reese and slid his arms around her from behind. "I'm sorry. Wyatt and Trace are more than partners to me. They're like brothers. They have an open invitation to come here."

She turned in his arms. "That's okay. Baby's cute. He's the guy you were telling me about the other night."

Cade leaned down and kissed her. "He is."

"And he looks like he needs a break."

"He does. But I'd much rather if it was just you and me here."

"I'll check my schedule. If my staff can continue to work without me, I'll add Sunday and Monday."

He pulled back. "Really?"

"Sure." She winced. "I'm starting to ~~feel~~ like I never want to go home. Which shoul~~d~~ make me get my butt onto that plane before I abandon my common sense. But what's two more days?"

He placed a smacking kiss on her lips. "Two more days will be perfect." Especially since Darcy napped a lot and sleep-deprived daddy Wyatt usually napped on the bed beside her crib. Even with them here, he and Reese would have plenty of alone time... And if they didn't, they could always go out on the boat.

Technically, Wyatt had gotten him two more days with Reese. He should be thanking him.

Cade headed for the refrigerator. "Okay, I'll make the eggs and bacon. How about if you toast some bagels."

"Sure."

She put bagels into the toaster, then retrieved dishes from the cabinet. She set them in front of the chairs by the kitchen island. The toaster popped and she raced back to get the bagels. She did that three or four times while Cade fried bacon and scrambled eggs with green peppers and onions.

By the time Wyatt appeared with his little girl decked out in a bright red one-piece swimsuit, a sunhat and oversize white sunglasses, everything was waiting for him.

"This is nice." He walked to the closet and pulled out a high chair, which he dragged to the center island.

Cade leaned in to whisper to Reese. "He stores a lot of stuff here. There are cribs in two of the bedrooms."

"I have to ride a bike from the helicopter pad. If I didn't leave stuff here, I'd look like a circus clown peddling down your path with all her things on my back."

Reese said, "Makes sense," then dug into her breakfast, making Cade hide a laugh, remembering that just the day before she'd said she wasn't a breakfast person. "I'll have to call my staff this morning to make sure our schedule can handle me taking two more days off."

"What's the point in owning a business if you can't take time off?" Wyatt asked as he picked up his fork to begin eating. "We don't exactly come and go as we please, but Cade, Trace and I aren't slaves to the jobs. We like our fun."

Cade glanced at her. "It's true."

She shook her head, then laughed. "I know how hard you guys work. How dedicated you are."

"Which makes us all the more determined to have fun," Cade said.

She picked up her fork again. "You two are crazy, you know that?"

Cade said, "Yes," as Wyatt said, "Absolutely."

"I'll call my staff when we're done eating."

After breakfast Reese went to the den down the hall to call her administrative assistant and her assistant manager to get the scoop on her clients. Cleaning the kitchen, Cade laid down a few ground rules for Wyatt.

"Number one, give us our privacy."

Readjusting dark-haired, blue-eyed Darcy so he required only one hand to hold her on his lap as he fed her a bottle, Wyatt said, "Of course."

"Number two, don't interfere. I know that in our company we complement each other. That everybody has their own specialty, so we count on each other. But, seriously, when it comes to romance, I'm okay on my own."

"Whatever you say. You'll hardly know we're here." Wyatt handed him the baby. "Take her. I've got to set up her umbrella and her baby pool."

Accustomed to helping Wyatt with Darcy when he brought her to the office, Cade easily slid the little girl into his arms. "You have a baby pool?"

"Shows how much you pay attention. That and her beach umbrella are in the cabana."

He settled Darcy on his arm. "Okay."

Wyatt left and Cade looked down at the

beautiful little girl. "How are you ever going to stay sane with that guy as your role model?"

Darcy giggled as if she'd understood him.

"I'm telling you. He's overprotective and bossy."

Reese entered the room on a laugh. "You could be describing yourself."

"No," Cade said. "I have caveman moments. He has a god complex."

She strolled over.

Cade continued, "Which is why he really does need breaks. He takes the baby places like this where he's got the peace and privacy to work and care for her without the stress of worrying that having a baby around is bothering other workers."

"He doesn't seem like the kind to care about something like that."

"He does. He seems all casual and nonchalant, but he had a weird upbringing. Rich dad. Mom who ran the society pages. He pretends to be cool and not give a damn what anyone thinks but he's always watching."

Reese said, "Hmm," reached for her mug from that morning and began making a second cup of coffee. "Doesn't he have a nanny?"

Cade rolled his eyes. "He's had nannies. I think the last count was seven. And he's fired them all. I don't know what he's looking for in a caregiver, but so far he hasn't found it."

She took Darcy from Cade's arms and nuzzled her. "Maybe he just likes being with her."

"They have sort of been joined at the hip since the night his ex dropped her off."

She nuzzled Darcy again. "Babies always smell so good."

"Since when do you go around sniffing babies?"

"Nurses care for people. My company's helped out a new mom or two."

He studied her as she gooed and cooed at the little girl, who looked like she was trying to talk. He'd never seen anyone as sweet or angelic with a baby as Reese was.

He remembered when he got engaged to Brenda. Back then, he'd thought that he'd wanted kids. Those feelings rose up in him again, but he dismissed them with the logic he'd had the day before. He was very successful and very happy with the status quo.

"You should take the job as Wyatt's nanny."

She laughed, lifted the little girl and blew on her belly. "Not on your life. Live in Manhattan? Give up the dream of expanding my business—"

Wyatt walked into the kitchen. "Who's expanding a business?"

"Me. Maybe. Eventually."

"I told her to franchise," Cade said. "She doesn't want to be only a manager. She likes the nursing part."

Wyatt grunted as he washed his hands. "Too bad. Franchises done right can be gold mines."

Cade bent toward Reese and whispered, "He could do most of the business plan for you in a few hours of his spare time."

"I don't have any spare time," Wyatt said. "I have a baby."

He reached for Darcy, but Reese held her away. "Are you kidding? She's adorable and happy and we're going to play in the water, aren't we, sweetie?"

Wyatt said, "Are you sure?"

"Yes! Go... Hey, maybe you and Cade could take the boat out and fish?"

Wyatt slid a sideways glance at Cade, who gave him a cold, hard stare.

"Nah. No fishing today. But I wouldn't mind being able to have a beer or two."

Cade balked. "It's morning!"

Wyatt shrugged. "It's vacation. Seriously, I never get to have a beer anymore. I have to be awake and alert because I'm the one caring for Darcy."

Reese laughed. "Have a beer. Have a few. When she's tired, I can put her down for a nap."

Wyatt smirked at Cade, who shook his head. But he knew his friend needed a break and he had to admit there was something about seeing Reese with Darcy that gave him a mushy feeling in the pit of his stomach.

He reminded himself of his first marriage, reminded himself that Reese had her own goals, and the feelings went away.

After Reese slathered Darcy with sunblock and Wyatt found her sunhat on the kitchen floor where it had fallen during breakfast, she and the baby played in the pool. She marveled at the little girl's resilience. She'd essentially been abandoned by her mom and given to a dad who was only learning to care for a baby. Yet she happily splashed in the water and babbled about nothing as Reese played with her.

Her heart unexpectedly swelled with longing to be a mom, to have a family. She could see herself bringing her own little brood to a beach house, teaching them to swim, teaching them about the ocean, about waves that moved in and tickled their toes and then raced out again.

She quickly squelched the vision along with the need that tightened her chest and sent a keen yearning singing through her veins. Tony's reaction to her not being able to have kids had been humiliating. There was no way

on God's green earth she'd risk telling another man she couldn't have kids. No way she
wanted to see that look of disappointment and
endure the sense that she wasn't good enough.

She shook off the memory. Her life might not
be perfect, but it was hers and it was the right
life. There was meaning and purpose in helping people. Her employees were her friends.
Her clients were her friends. She was a part
of her community. Lots of people had far less.
Jobs they disliked. No meaning or purpose in
their work.

And she did get to play with babies. They
popped up in her world all the time.

She had a lot to be thankful for.

She took Darcy out of the water and sat with
her under the big blue, coral and lime green
beach umbrella to play, making sure the baby
didn't get too much sun and simply enjoying
the sweet little bundle of joy.

Wyatt swam, got a beer, then sat at a patio
table with Cade, talking business, high-level
stuff that perked up Reese's ears and filled
her with curiosity, but mostly went over her
head. Partly because she was only half listening. Partly because the amounts of money they
so casually threw around were astronomical.

Darcy grew tired after a second time in the
pool and Reese fed her a bottle, took her up-

stairs, put her into tiny pajamas and rocked her. She cradled the baby like the precious bundle that she was, watching her blue eyes drift closed.

As she laid her in the crib, the pull to linger and simply stare at her tiny face filled Reese. Though it was wrong, she let herself pretend— just for a second—that this was her baby, her child to mother and protect and love with all her heart. The yearning tripled and a sense of loss flooded her but she shook her head to get rid of it.

She'd long ago learned to appreciate what she *did* have and accept what she didn't. She'd built a happy life for herself. So why, suddenly, did her heart keep softening with longing?

Because of Cade?

She frowned as she thought about that. Sixteen-year-old Reese and eighteen-year-old Cade *had* made plans—detailed plans—for the future. They'd wanted a big house, a brood of strawberry blonds, laughter and connection. *He'd* wanted a family. A real family. He'd wanted all the things she'd had with parents who behaved like real parents. He'd wanted to play games with his kids, go to their football games and cheer for them when they played soccer. He'd wanted to steer them to the right university. To counsel them about life. To have *that* connection.

And now he didn't?

In a way that didn't make sense.

At eighteen, he'd been consumed by the need to have his own family, to raise his kids with patience and love, and his just dropping that vision didn't seem right.

Of course, he'd endured a terrible divorce and he'd made a good life for himself too. Just as she had—

No, that wasn't entirely true. She hadn't *decided* to let go of the dream of getting pregnant, having kids. Fate had chosen for her. And it hadn't been easy to accept it. For a while, she'd considered a few options for creating a family. Adoption. In vitro. But Tony's reaction had been so bad that she'd known she'd never be able to get close enough to another man to risk telling him. To risk not merely another heartbreak but also the humiliation of being told he didn't love her enough to take an alternative path.

So she'd accepted her infertility and found another way to have a good life.

Cade's story was entirely different. Losing a marriage shouldn't have made him decide not to have kids—

She shook her head to clear those thoughts.

For all practical intents and purposes, she and Cade were having a vacation fling. She shouldn't be thinking too deeply about his life. About what he wanted and what he didn't want.

She took one final look at the baby, letting her teenage dreams with Cade drift off into nothing, then pulled away.

Finding a baby monitor on the dresser beside the crib, she brought it down to the pool and set it on an available table. "We'll hear her if she fusses."

Wyatt said, "Thanks."

"You're welcome."

"You wouldn't happen to want to be a really well-paid nanny, would you?"

"Already told Cade I don't want to live in Manhattan."

Cade said, "It's true."

She eased down to sit on the edge of the pool, dangling her feet in the cool water. Wanting to help Wyatt, she said, "But I wouldn't mind giving you a hand finding a new nanny."

Wyatt peered at her. "You could do that?"

"Sure. I interview nurses and caregivers all the time. I know more than qualifications count. I look for certain personality traits."

Wyatt beamed. "Exactly."

"Great. We can do video chat interviews. Send me some résumés of candidates you like, and I'll have my assistant set them up when we get back home."

"Or," Wyatt said, "how about if I call my assistant now and have her set up second interviews from the batch of people I talked to this week, then we can do the video calls this afternoon."

"You have some candidates?"

"Yes. Three or four seem great. But having been burned by seven, I'm a bit gun-shy."

Reese laughed and walked to a chaise to stretch out. "Have her organize the second interviews for this afternoon and I'll sit in. We'll make the decision together."

Wyatt reached for his phone. "I would appreciate that."

Reese said, "I'm happy to do it," then settled into the chaise, her normal self again. She enjoyed helping people. *That* was her thing. She didn't fret about what she didn't have or couldn't do. She didn't overexamine other people's motives and decisions, like Cade's. She focused on the positive.

As Wyatt walked into the house for quiet to call his assistant, Cade came over and plopped down on the chaise beside her.

"He found our stash of no-bakes."

"The cookies?" Reese laughed as she faced him. Their gazes connected and her heart thrummed. He was so handsome and so normal. No pretense. Just a very smart guy who was making the best of his life just as she had. There was no reason to dig any deeper.

"Putting them in the freezer wasn't exactly hiding them," Cade continued, shaking his head. "But he ate them frozen."

"Barbarian!"

Cade laughed. "He *is* a barbarian."

She laughed too, glad they had this happy, easy connection.

He rose from his chaise, held his hand out to her. "Let's go take a walk on the beach."

"That's a great idea." She took the hand he offered. "For as many days as we've been here, we haven't walked on the beach!" When she got her balance in front of him, she leaned in and kissed him. "I can't think of anything I'd rather do."

She smiled but the sense that something was wrong with this picture suddenly hummed along her nerve endings. For a second she wondered if they both weren't merely pretending to be happy, settling for less than what they'd always wanted together.

But she quieted those thoughts. Twelve years had gone by since they'd created those silly dreams. Circumstances were different now. Cade no longer wanted to get married, admitting he'd also dropped his desire to have a family. That's what she needed to focus on.

Especially since what they had might not last beyond this week.

For the next few days, she would simply make him happy and be happy herself, as she put their silly teenage dreams in a box and locked it.

CHAPTER ELEVEN

REESE AND WYATT spent the afternoon by the pool videoconferencing with nanny candidates. Cade entertained himself by swimming, walking down to the dock and being the one to retrieve Darcy when she woke.

At five, when the video interviews were still going strong, he pulled the high chair out to the patio, put the baby in and started grilling pork loin and veggies.

They ate at six, with Reese and Wyatt discussing the contenders for the job as Darcy's caregiver. At eight, Wyatt put the baby to bed, but he was back with the monitor to continue the nanny discussions.

Cade raised the TV from the stone counter and set it to watch a movie. Reese and Wyatt made second calls to two of the interviewees, needing to ask a few more questions for clarification. Wyatt was a billionaire. His child was a potential target for kidnappers. His penthouse was a treasure trove of art. They had to take all that into consideration when they chose his nanny.

Rolling his eyes, Cade shifted on his chaise lounge. He'd never seen Wyatt take this long to make a decision. The guy was a risk taker. But right now, all he was taking was Cade's girl. How could two simple clarification calls take *hours*?

The movie finished and, tired and bored, Cade announced that he was going to his room.

Reese chirped, "Good night!" But Wyatt only grunted.

A bit annoyed, he undressed and showered with all fourteen jets pulsing around him. His feeling of abandonment like raw sores, he spent longer under the spray than usual. He knew he was being childish, particularly since Wyatt would be leaving in another day. But memories of Reese refusing to talk to him after she broke up with him lingered. He now knew why. She'd suffered a terrible trauma—and hadn't been able to confide in him. When the chips were down, she'd leaned on her parents, which—given her age—was the right thing to do.

Unfortunately, even that good logic didn't stop the recollection of how alone he was those weeks when he went back to Harvard after that Thanksgiving. Losing her had resulted in him bonding with Trace and Wyatt. But in the back of his brain the loss had lingered. Even at eighteen, he'd known what they'd had was special. Important. Losing it so abruptly, with little explanation, had left him adrift and empty.

Of course, not knowing what had really happened, he'd also assumed she'd ditched him for someone else and had eventually concluded what they'd had hadn't been real. Just a bunch of hormones and entertainment.

But what if it hadn't been?

What if it had been real?

Brenda's image popped into his brain. He'd married her because she fit his life. At the time, he'd assumed the way she'd eased into his penthouse, his charity events, his bed meant he loved her. But he'd never had extraordinary feelings for her. He'd simply wanted to fill a spot, be married, start a family.

Because he'd always wanted a family. No matter how he tried to tell himself he'd satisfied that need by having friends who were like brothers, he couldn't deny his longing to be a dad.

The truth of that was like a splash of cold water. Was that why he'd had those feelings watching Reese with Darcy? Had seeing them together reminded him of everything he'd wanted as a kid?

Did he want those things again?

With Reese?

He stepped out of the shower and grabbed a towel, scolding himself. All this stuff rolling around in his brain was the result of having too much time on his hands because Wyatt had kept Reese busy.

He and Reese had both come to the island to have fun. Not to try to mend a relationship that had died twelve years ago. They also couldn't re-create the past. She'd suffered a trauma. He'd made foolish choices.

So, no.

No turning back. No thinking about the future.

When he finished drying and walked into the master bedroom again, he stopped.

Reese was in his bed. Asleep.

His heart turned over in his chest. Not only did she look exhausted from a morning of babysitting Darcy and an afternoon and evening of helping Wyatt find a nanny, but she'd come to his room. As naturally as if she belonged there.

He thought about foolish choices and long-ago dreams and shook his head, not letting himself go there again.

This is a vacation fling. Nothing more. She might belong in his bed for the next few days, but he wouldn't take his thoughts any further than that.

He slid beneath the covers as quietly as he could, so he wouldn't wake her. But her floral scent drifted to him. She'd showered too.

He closed his eyes and savored the sweet smells, disappointed that she hadn't come to his room to shower. If she had, she could have joined him.

Tomorrow, he'd tell her to bring her things to the master. Because she did belong here, and he wanted her here. It was part of the easy fun they were having.

Not a big deal.

He cuddled against her and fell into a deep, refreshing sleep, refusing to let his thoughts go any further than this day, this moment.

They woke at seven almost simultaneously and curled into each other for a long, thorough lovemaking session. They showered together and she slipped into the yoga pants and T-shirt she'd set on the chair in the corner of the room.

Downstairs, he made coffee. She made cinnamon toast, another simple but fun thing she knew how to make because of having a normal childhood.

Wyatt walked into the kitchen with Darcy strapped to his chest. "We're going to swim a bit, then pack up to leave."

Cade worked not to sound sarcastic when he said, "So soon?"

Wyatt laughed. "I'm back to being relaxed. Plus, I have a nanny coming tomorrow morning. I need to get home and prepare myself to orient nanny number eight."

Reese said, "Hey, she's great! And if she isn't, Peach Osgood was another good candidate."

Wyatt put Darcy in the high chair, fixed himself a cup of coffee and sat down at the island. Helping himself to some cinnamon toast, he said, "Seriously. Thank you so much for joining me on those interviews yesterday."

"Hiring a nanny is a lot like finding a good nurse. They have to have a heart for the job."

They drank their coffee and ate their cinnamon toast chatting about nothing, then Wyatt took the baby to her splashing pool. After tidying the kitchen, Reese and Cade strolled out to the patio. Reese sat at a table scrolling through texts and emails from her staff, as Cade played with Darcy while Wyatt looked on.

After lunch, Wyatt dressed Darcy in tiny jeans and a T-shirt, then came back downstairs to say goodbye. He headed to the garage to get a bike, but Cade said, "Wait. I'll come with you."

"Really?"

"Yeah. I'll stick your duffel bag in the basket of my bike and make things easier for you."

"Since when do you want to make things easier for me?"

Cade motioned for him to go to the garage. "Since always."

Wyatt settled himself on the bike, Darcy securely strapped to his chest. They headed off through the foliage.

"You spent a lot of time with Darcy yesterday and today."

Cade gaped at him. "I spend a lot of time with her every day! You're on a call. I'm holding the baby. You need to read something. I'm the one taking her to the window to look at the tall buildings."

Wyatt harrumphed. "Guess I got a nanny just in time."

"I'm not complaining. I like her."

"That was kind of what I was hinting at. I think your feelings about what you want out of life are changing. Not just because you like Darcy but I saw how possessive you were with Reese."

Cade balked. "What?"

Before Wyatt could answer, the sound of Dennis approaching in the helicopter filled the air.

Wyatt got off his bike and Cade reached for

it, shouting, "I'll put your bike away. You get the duffel off mine."

Wyatt nodded. Cade put Wyatt's bike in the outbuilding. The helicopter got closer and closer, the noise almost deafening.

Still, when Cade returned, Wyatt shouted, "Don't ignore what I said about what you want out of life. If Reese is changing you, make sure it's not just nostalgia."

Cade held back a sputter of indignation. He'd already figured out what Wyatt had said. He didn't need to be reminded that he didn't really want all those old dreams with Reese. Or to be told it was only nostalgia edging him in that direction. He wouldn't say or do anything foolish. He'd learned that lesson long ago.

Unfortunately, with the slowing helicopter blades still making noise, he couldn't get into this with Wyatt now. So he simply said, "She lives in Ohio. I live in Manhattan. Neither one of us would ever move to the other's city. We're both fulfilled in our careers. We know what we're doing."

The helicopter blades finally stopped. Wyatt slapped Cade's shoulder. "Okay. Great." Then he ran toward the waiting vehicle, Darcy on his chest, duffel bag over his shoulder.

Cade waved goodbye, watching them. Wyatt was gruff. His current living arrangement was busy. But there was a happiness, a contentment about him that would have made him tease Wyatt, except he was happy too.

At least until Monday afternoon. Or Tuesday morning. Whichever Reese decided was the end of their trip.

His heart dipped with disappointment that his time with Reese was running out, but he shook his head to clear it. Now that he had everything figured out, he wasn't ruining it by giving in to unwanted, unwarranted longings for things he'd long ago decided weren't right for him.

He did not want to think about the future. He and Reese had both come to the island for rest and relaxation. Nothing more serious was happening.

The helicopter took off and Cade got back on his bike. In ten minutes, he was storing it in the garage and walking to the patio, where Reese lay stretched out on a chaise by the pool.

Her long limbs were an interesting shade of reddish brown. Not sunburned, but on their way to tan. "How come a redhead like you isn't all sunburned?"

She didn't even open her eyes. "Sunblock."

"You can get tan through sunblock?"

"Sure. Though it takes a few days."

And they'd been there for six days. Mostly

outside. He glanced around. They were always on the patio because it was beautiful.

Paradise.

Usually when he had thoughts like these, he was on the beach. He turned to ask Reese if she wanted to go for a walk with him, but she looked comfortable and he was determined to stay away from confusing thinking so he only said, "I'm going for a walk on the beach."

He left the statement open, giving her a chance to decide if she wanted to go with him.

She said, "Okay," didn't ask or offer to come along and seemed content just as she was. Because they weren't two peas in a pod. They weren't joined at the hip. They weren't resurrecting a "once in a lifetime" thing. They were two friends, who had become lovers. Again. They'd done this before, and the last time had ended miserably. This time, they would be able to walk away with neither one of them getting hurt.

He left her alone, ambling down the path that led to the sandy beach. He walked a few minutes, picking up shells to see how far he could throw them from the shore. But after a few throws that got boring.

He glanced up at the patio, where Reese lay, soaking up sun, knowing the walk would have been so much more fun if she'd joined him.

An itchy, weird feeling slithered through him. For a second, he wondered if he would no longer be happy on this island if she wasn't with him, but it was so preposterous that he let it go and waded into the blue water until it was waist high, then he dived in.

After twenty minutes of swimming, he walked back to the patio, found a towel and rubbed it over his dripping hair.

She opened one eye. "We should play Yahtzee."

He laughed. "Yahtzee?"

"Yeah. I fell asleep twice and I'm starting to worry that I won't sleep tonight if I don't get up."

He sat sideways on the chaise beside hers. He didn't like the thoughts he'd been having on the beach. But instead of fighting the fear that the island wouldn't be as much fun without her, he'd come up with a workaround. He'd figured out a way to compartmentalize everything he was feeling, to have it make sense, so it fit.

"Did you ever stop to think you need the rest?" She peeked over at him. "Maybe."

"Then you should take time off a couple times a year. It's why I have this place. Why Wyatt and Trace have an open invitation to come here. When you're in charge of as much money as we play with, there's stress. Not because we worry about going broke, but because we employ thousands of people. They count on us to provide wages, benefits."

She sat up. "That's it exactly. My job's not difficult. My employees are great. But I am responsible to make sure they get a paycheck. After five years of no time off, I think it got to me."

Satisfied that he was on the right track, he chuckled. "Probably. I'll add you to the invitation list. Give me your email and once a month when the code to open the house changes, you'll get the new one. You don't have to check in to see if anyone's here because there are five bedrooms. In fact, Trace, Wyatt and I have had some of our best times when we surprised each other, and all came here at the same time."

She glanced up at him with a smile. "So, I'm part of the in crowd."

He rose. "I think you earned that honor when you helped Wyatt find a nanny."

Her smile grew into a grin. "It's like I'm in a secret society."

Having officially categorized her as friend with the open invitation to the island, there was no more confusion in his mind about what was going on between them.

He bent and kissed her forehead. "Yeah. You're happy now but wait until it sinks in for

Wyatt that you could franchise. He'll be at your door at two o'clock in the morning someday, with a fifty-page business plan."

She laughed.

"I'm serious. You helped him. He won't rest until he helps you." He took a long breath and glanced around. He thought about her request to play Yahtzee. When she'd gotten here, she'd seemed interested in touring the islands, but every time he'd been at the house, she'd been here. He didn't think she'd ever gone over on her own to sightsee. She'd certainly never requested he drive her there.

She always had been shy about asking for things, about getting her own way, which was probably the result of being one of three kids, not an only child, as he was.

This was another thing he could fix.

"Do you really want to play Yahtzee, or would you rather tour the islands?"

She straightened a little more on the chaise. "Actually, a tour of the islands sounds fabulous."

He headed for the door. "Go get dressed. Shorts. T-shirt. Flip-flops. Don't embarrass me by looking like a tourist."

She laughed, but he turned suddenly, another thought striking him. She'd spent their last two days like a vagabond. Changing in her room and sleeping in his. He'd already decided he would ask her to bring her things to his room. This seemed like the perfect time.

"Why don't you bring your suitcase to my room?"

"Right now?"

"Yeah. Thanks to Wyatt, we have two more days. It just seems inconvenient for you to dress in one room and sleep in another."

She frowned, as if she couldn't understand what he was asking.

He groaned. "Come on. Don't tease. We're having fun. Bring your things to the master. Make both of our lives easier."

She gathered her clothes and cosmetics and carried them to the master suite. By the time she got there, the room was empty. The shower was still warm from Cade getting ready for their tour of the islands, but he was nowhere around.

She set her things on the marble countertop of the double sinks, an odd sensation moving through her.

Sleeping in his room was one thing. Having her toiletries beside his felt so permanent— so weirdly like a step she didn't want to take. Almost as if she had given him the wrong impression—

She liked the idea that he thought of her

as one of his friends. Like Wyatt and Trace. Someone with whom he would share his island. It was a way of being in his life without being in his life. But she hoped he wasn't thinking anything more was going on. If he believed things were happening between them that shouldn't—that *couldn't*—then they'd have to have that awkward conversation. The one she didn't want to have with *anyone* ever again.

She showered telling herself not to go overboard. So he was giving her access to his island? She might think it was a big deal. But he didn't. As he'd said, billionaires had better toys. They were the ones who *should* share.

She showered and dressed, then returned downstairs to find Cade on the patio talking with Trace on the phone. When he flashed the phone to her, gathering her image for Trace, she smiled and waved. "Hey, Trace."

"I told him you now have access to the house anytime you want."

She stopped halfway to a chaise lounge.

She'd teased him that granting her access was like bringing her into a secret club, but hearing him announce it to Trace felt weird—

Significant—

That's what had been bothering her. *Significance.* It was significant to be sharing his suite. Now, he had told his friend she had an open invitation to come to his island. Add those two together and it felt like they were becoming a couple.

She stopped that thought, reminding herself that his world was abundantly different from hers, the way he thought about things was different. He considered this house much more than the vacation home she saw. To him it was a sanctuary. Not merely for himself. For his friends too. He clearly considered her a friend.

Plus, at no time had he ever mentioned that he would be at the beach house when she was.

She was reading into things only because being with Darcy had reminded her of their old dreams. But those dreams couldn't come true. And they had a mere two more days on the island. She needed to get back into relaxation mode and stop thinking!

He disconnected his call and took her hand. They walked down the path to the dock, he helped her into the boat and—without as much as a nudge from her—he slid into his life vest. She forced herself not to make a big deal of that. He was being a smart boater. Nothing more.

They traveled a bit north, edging in close to the islands so she could see the highway that connected them, then they headed south again.

"I thought we'd spend time on Key West."

"Okay."

"I want you to see Mallory Square." He peeked back at her. "There's shopping and restaurants, plus street performers and a gorgeous view of the sunset. Not to mention chickens who roam the streets."

"Chickens?"

"Yep. Real chickens. Gives a whole new meaning to *free range*."

She laughed, her apprehensions easing. "Sounds nice."

"*Nice?* It's amazing. And that's why I like the Keys." He pointed east. "I can be over there, on my own private retreat when I want peace and quiet. Or come over here—" he pointed at Key West, which grew increasingly larger as they approached it "—when I want to have fun. Mingle. Get a beer with overenthusiastic tourists."

"Okay. That sounds…" Not like a guy who wanted commitments. But a guy who liked his freedom. Which relaxed her even more. "…like tons of fun."

"It is!"

Their easy conversation went a long way to remind her that he was a happy-go-lucky person. Plus, they'd only just found each other after twelve long years. They'd spent a week together. *A week.* He wasn't asking her to be his girlfriend. They weren't in a relationship. He'd asked her to move into his room because they were sleeping together, having fun. As he'd said, it was simple convenience.

They docked at the island and she removed her vest. He took her hand again and led her into a thickening crowd.

"This is their sunset festival."

She looked around. Sea air and heat enveloped everything. "Festival?"

"Every day about two hours before sunset, there's a little informal celebration." He pointed to where a crowd was gathering. "Most times that I've been here there's been juggling, a one-man band, a magician…and a guy who has house cats who do tricks."

She giggled. "House cats who do tricks? I can't even get my cat to lift her head when I get home from work."

"His cats are great. It's actually pretty funny."

"Can't wait to see it." She really couldn't. He'd taken their situation from strained to natural with a simple boat ride and a walk around the crowded island.

He let her watch the performances to her heart's delight, then got them seated in the best place to see the sunset from one of the outdoor restaurants.

They ate shrimp talking about everything from the wonder of Mallory Square to Wyatt's misspent childhood.

"I think he's making up for that now."

"To his parents?"

"Yes. He impresses his dad with his ability to make money and his mother by staying out of the society pages."

"If she's a true society lady, I would think she'd want him *in* the society pages."

"The only times he's ever made it was for bad behavior. Drunk at gallery openings and fundraisers."

Reese winced. "Yikes." She thought for a second, then said, "He doesn't drink much now."

"Nope. He wasn't ever an alcoholic. He was more like lost. Once we found our niche, he found purpose."

"He isn't just making money to impress his dad?"

"Started out that way. Now he loves it."

He paid for their dinners using a bank card but put down cash for a healthy tip. "This way the waitress gets the money immediately."

"Funny that you should know that."

"My ex had been a waitress."

Mellowed by the once-again easy conversation between them, she slid her arm beneath his and nestled against him as they made the slow return walk to his boat. "Really? Why did I think you'd married a stockbroker or banker?"

He snorted. "From the way she tried to get part of my company?"

"Maybe."

Perfection floated on the air with the scents of coconut sunblock and the sea. It followed them home on the boat ride and up the path from the dock to the patio.

He opened the house with a few taps on the security pad by the kitchen door and they walked inside, through the kitchen and up the stairs to the master.

As soon as they entered, he took her in his arms. "I love having you here."

She couldn't tell if he was talking about having her with him on the island or in the master. But she didn't let herself overthink it. She loved being here. Both on the island with him and in his most private domain. She desperately wanted the rest of the time they had left to be happy. She didn't want to think about things that didn't matter in a vacation fling.

She shoved them out of her mind and stepped nearer. "I love being here."

He gave her lips a chaste brush, then the innocent kiss deepened. Contentment spread through her. Tingles warmed her spine. With a nudge of his palm against the small of her back, he pressed her closer. Then his hands roamed up her back, and down again, so he could slide them under the hem of her tank top. His nimble fingers found her bra closure and released it, before gliding to her breasts.

She groaned and stepped back, allowing him to strip away the tank top and bra. Before bringing her close again, he removed his shirt.

Her hands slid to the muscles of his shoulders. For a few seconds, the sheer joy of getting to touch him again, kiss him again, nearly overwhelmed her. She basked in that sensation as they kissed and touched some more before their shorts began to feel like an unwanted barrier and had to go.

Then they tumbled to the bed. His bed. Big and luxurious, it was a sort of symbol of his wealth, his privilege. But she knew that no matter how smart he was, how hardnosed he was about business, he was still a guy who liked to have fun.

With a quick shove to his shoulder, she toppled him to his side of the bed and straddled him.

"What's this?"

"You said you liked me better bold and adventurous."

He chuckled. "Just how bold do you plan to get?"

She pretended to ponder that. "Why don't we wait and see?"

With that she bent and ran her tongue along his collarbone to his chest. He slid his hands up her back. There was something about the combination of *them*. Something that made every touch, every caress, sizzle. They teased and tempted each other to a breaking point, then he shifted their positions, flipping her to her back, and entered her.

Electricity crackled through her and she moaned at the sensation. So did he. Outside the wind picked up. The first signs of a storm. But safe and happy, they ignored it.

He fell asleep before she did, and she turned in his arms to simply look at him. His face was perfect. Angles and planes arranged to create high cheekbones and a strong jaw.

Sated, content, she had the sense that this was the way it was supposed to have been. That they weren't supposed to have lost each other. That they *were* supposed to click like two puzzle pieces. That Finn McCully's sin somehow threw a monkey wrench in fate's plans and ruined the life they were supposed to have.

Except—

If Cade hadn't left his parents to go to

school, would he have met the two friends who became his brothers? Would he have become rich? Would he be the mature, logical, strong guy she was falling in love with?

She drifted closer to him. Would she love being with the Cade who would have resulted if they'd stayed together?

Or would they have grown apart? After all, without that night, she would have studied political science and headed for the office of a congressman or senator in Washington, DC.

If he'd stayed in Ohio, he would still be refereeing his parents' fights.

Would she and Cade have become two entirely different people?

Worse, would they have drifted apart when she'd been told she couldn't have kids? When his dream of having a family changed?

She shuddered to think about it. How much harder would it have been to have lost him the way she'd lost Tony? Tony had adored her but he couldn't stay with her because she couldn't give him the family he wanted, the way he wanted. If she thought she'd suffered from feelings of being incomplete—not good enough—just plain not *enough*, when Tony dumped her, how much worse would it have been to have lost Cade that way?

She shook off the feeling. But she couldn't

get rid of her concern that their relationship wouldn't stop at the end of their stay. There was a good chance they'd visit the island at the same time. And then what? The more time they spent together, the more they could tiptoe toward really falling in love. And if not love, toward growing close enough to drift into deep discussions. She didn't want to be drawn into conversations that would lead her to tell him she couldn't have kids. She didn't want to disappoint him.

Still, part of her wished he would be with her every time she came to the island. That part wished they'd swim and eat no-bakes. Make love in the pool. Laugh a lot. Never be serious. Play Yahtzee and go for boat rides, but never want more.

The hollowness of that wish rolled over her. Was this really what she wanted? A permanent hookup?

She slid away from Cade, thrashing a bit to find a position that was comfortable, and failing. What seemed like the perfect arrangement—what *was* the perfect arrangement—was empty.

But what was the alternative?

A real relationship?

Telling him her deepest secret? Watching his expression change when she admitted that she couldn't have kids? Hearing him say he didn't want her?

She didn't want to go there with Cade. Didn't want to see the pity in his eyes that she'd seen in Tony's. Didn't want to have to watch him struggle through a period of indecision until he eventually slid out of her life. Or stayed in it and compromised. Meeting her only at the beach house. Never taking them beyond playing in the pool together.

When she was working, running her company, living her life as a vital part of her small town, she was enough. She was *more* than enough. She had a place. A future. It had taken years of work to get there. She wouldn't risk her hard-won self-respect and dignity.

Especially since he'd said he didn't want anything more.

He didn't want anything more.

She didn't want anything more.

As long as she didn't overthink this, they would be fine.

The only problem was... She couldn't stop thinking.

CHAPTER TWELVE

CADE WOKE SATURDAY morning to find Reese gone. He jumped out of bed and into shorts and a T-shirt and raced downstairs, worried that she'd packed up, intending to leave. After all, she was supposed to stay only a week and yesterday had marked seven whole days they'd been on the island.

Wyatt had extended their stay, but Cade had felt the difference in her the night before. He hadn't been able to come up with the words to ask why she'd rolled away from him and kept tossing and turning. Maybe because it seemed foolish to say, "Hey, why are you restless?"

It also seemed intrusive. Particularly when the urge to ask her kept getting stronger. He liked her. He didn't want to see her unhappy. And he'd sensed there was something really bothering her.

Still, they'd been together only a week and the desperate need he had to take care of her was wrong. As Wyatt said, it was nostalgia. Plus, it took them to emotional places neither one of them wanted to go.

So, no. He hadn't asked her why she'd been tossing and turning. Thanks to Wyatt they had two more days on the island. Only two days. Surely, he could keep his feelings from going too far for two days.

Of course he could. As Wyatt had said, part of what he felt for her was an echo of what he'd felt in the past. Their being together had an air of picking up where they left off. But they weren't. They couldn't. They were two different people now.

Recognizing that, he would control himself. Not make something out of nothing.

Unfortunately, he still didn't know why she'd been restless the night before.

He found her in the kitchen, mixing batter. "What are you making?"

She grinned at him. "Muffins."

He cautiously eased to the center island. "Really?"

"There was a boxed mix in your cupboard." She held up an odd pan of some sort. "And see? Here's a muffin tin."

Radiating happiness, she did not look like a woman who hadn't been able to sleep because of something important the night before. So maybe she'd simply had trouble finding a comfortable position?

The first stirrings of relief tiptoed into his tight chest. "What kind of muffins am I getting?"

"Banana nut."

His stomach stilled. "I love those."

"Clearly someone knows that because the boxed mix was right there." She pointed at a cabinet.

He took a seat on one of the stools in front of the island. He was getting muffins and Reese was behaving normally. Whatever had made her restless the night before was gone.

But here came the real test. "Wanna fish with me this morning?"

"You mean, do I want to rest on the boat while *you* fish?"

"You could bring a book."

She laughed. "I have a ton I can read on my phone. In fact—" She chewed her lower lip as if she were thinking. "Maybe I'll listen to an audiobook."

He reached to take a taste of the batter, but she swatted his fingers away.

"It's quiet enough out there that you could certainly listen to a book."

"Audiobook it is."

She smiled at him and his nerve endings calmed completely. She would be going home

Tuesday morning or maybe even Monday night. He refused to mar their time together with worry or pointless speculation. From here on out, it was nothing but fun.

He got dressed to go out on the boat while the muffins baked, then ate two reading his phone on the patio while she dressed. He held her hand as they walked down to the dock and put on a life vest when she did. Except this time when he closed the catches on hers, he kissed her for every catch, teasing her, making her laugh.

She put her earbuds in and settled on the bench seat, closing her eyes as she listened to her book. For Cade, the whole world righted. As she listened and he fished, he thought about how nice it was to be with her, to have her in his life again, and was glad he'd decided to give her the codes to the house. To keep her in his life.

Because they were friends. Maybe not in a real relationship. But definitely friends. He would never even tiptoe toward making what they had a relationship. His marriage had been a disaster. Brenda wanted things he couldn't give. Not gifts or money. But time. It was as if she didn't understand the concept of work. Didn't understand he had goals and responsibilities—

Though Reese did. Mostly because she had those same issues, goals and responsibilities.

Still, they lived in different states. Different worlds. Even dating wasn't an option. He could visit her in Ohio, but he hated Ohio. She could visit him in New York... But he'd much rather they both flew to the island when they wanted to see each other.

He'd already given her access to the beach house. He could easily tempt her to the island a few times a year. They could enjoy each other's company and not risk what they had with talks of making it into something neither of them wanted.

He caught a few fish but when he was done for the morning, he realized she was fast asleep.

Laughing at her, he nudged her butt with his foot. "Get up, sleepyhead."

She bounced up, saw where she was, looked at her phone and groaned. "Damn! I'm going to have to backtrack to try to figure out where I drifted off."

"Maybe the book was boring?"

She shook her head. "No. The book is great. I just feel like I can't get enough sleep."

"You work too hard." But thoughts of her tossing and turning the night before returned. He could ask why, but wasn't that going a step too far? Making more of what they were doing than they should?

He finished putting away his fishing gear.

"Maybe you don't sleep enough at home? Most people who come down here spend the days fishing and the nights on the island partying. You've had the most low-key vacation of anyone I know."

Her head tilted and she smiled at him. "It didn't seem to bother you."

He leaned in and kissed her. "No. It did not."

They took a slow, scenic route back to his island. She stood beside him at the helm, asking a million questions about how to drive the boat and he happily answered them. He liked watching her get familiar with the cruiser, his island. Her interest said she would come back. By herself sometimes. But also, he could have Dennis call him when she came for some R&R. He wouldn't join her every time, but enough times that eventually he could call her and ask her to come with him when he was coming down for a rest. No pressure on either one of them. Just the way he liked it.

Happy that things were working out, they held hands walking up the path from the dock. When they reached the patio, he stopped and looked around.

"What's different?"

Confused, Reese repeated his movements, her gaze inching around the pool area. Their fishing trip had been just like the first one—nothing different there. The storm the night before had knocked a few palm fronds to the ground but in a way that was normal here on the island.

"I don't see anything…"

He laughed, then leaned down and kissed her. "Maybe it's that you're here. I like having you here. I like *you*. It's so easy and comfortable."

She peeked at him, totally unsure why he thought he had to spell that out.

He dropped her hand and walked toward the grill. "I'm thinking we'll have hamburgers for lunch."

Reese said, "It's three."

Cade shrugged. "I made dinner reservations for eight thirty tonight. The sun will probably be setting as we take the boat over to the island. The view will be spectacular."

And romantic.

He'd timed it for her. He knew she loved the boat. He knew she loved the sunsets. The thought that he'd put into their dinner plans filled her heart, shot happiness through her—

Of course, he'd also said having her with him was easy and comfortable. Making dinner reservations was all part of keeping things organized, so they didn't get complicated.

"But that also means we won't be eating

until around nine. So, I'll grill some burgers for lunch."

She shook her head to clear it of too much thinking, and said, "Good idea." But the hollow feeling about what they were doing returned. She might have forced herself out of her doldrums from the night before, convincing herself that what they had was not a threat to her secrets, but she wasn't sure she liked this odd, empty feeling.

It was almost as if deciding that what they felt would go no further than this had ruined it. Almost as if she couldn't enjoy it if there was no future. Part of the fun of their relationship had been planning their future and looking forward to being together forever.

The very idea brought her up short. She couldn't have it both ways. Either she told him she wanted more, which meant she'd also have to tell him *all* her secrets. Or she enjoyed what they had. Period.

Knowing there was only one answer to that, she walked into the house to get the potato salad and iced tea.

After they ate the burgers, Reese backtracked in her audiobook, searching for the last portion she remembered, then she got comfortable on a chaise and put in her earbuds, intending to spend a few hours listening to her book.

But after about ten minutes, boredom overtook her. She found another book, this one a best-seller she'd been dying to read, but again, an antsy feeling skimmed her skin.

She watched Cade casually putter around, mostly tidying the patio area, getting rid of leaves and branches that had fallen in the storm the night before, and tears filled her eyes. Here she was, at the top of her game, with the man she'd always loved, on a tropical island. In most people's point of view, this was as good as it got.

So why did she want more?

Why couldn't she just enjoy this?

CHAPTER THIRTEEN

THAT EVENING, THEY TOOK the boat to the island. Cade let Reese steer for a few minutes, and she threw herself into the role with gusto, as they watched the setting sun. He didn't hesitate to take her hand as they strolled to the restaurant, but he didn't linger over the street performers the way they had the night before. She seemed nervous again. Unhappy. So out of sorts that it physically hurt him not to ask her what was wrong.

But that wasn't their deal. They weren't supposed to get any closer than they already were. As it was, they'd confided some fairly big things. He didn't want this to tumble into something neither one of them intended.

Which meant their conversation while they ate was slow, meaningless. A few times Reese tried revving things up, but he could see her heart wasn't in it. So they took the boat back to the island.

As they walked up the path to the patio, his

phone rang. Caller ID told him it was his father. He blew his breath out on a sigh, clicked to answer and said, "Hey, Dad."

Reese peered over at him with her first real laugh all night, and he rolled his eyes.

"What's up?"

"I thought you'd be home by now."

"Wyatt came down. Stole two of our days so we decided to add two days to our trip."

"Oh. Good."

"You don't sound like you think it's good."

"No. No. It's fine. It's just that your mom and the preacher called it quits."

He covered the phone's microphone, leaned toward Reese and whispered, "Mom and the preacher broke up."

"Damn. I lost ten bucks."

He laughed and put the phone to his ear again. "That's too bad."

"It is. She finally looked happy. I was hoping you'd be home to visit. You know. To cheer her up."

It still amazed him when his dad behaved kindly toward his mom, but he didn't want to jinx it by mentioning it. "We're leaving Monday night. Maybe Tuesday morning so, yeah, I'll pop in to see her."

His dad said, "Good. Good," but an odd tone wove through his voice.

"Everything okay with *you*?"

"Yeah. I'm great." He dropped his voice to a whisper. "Lila's here."

"Lila?"

Reese's eyebrows rose and his dad's voice lowered even more. "My nurse. We were on our way to the movie when the rumor about your mom hit."

Realizing why Reese's eyebrows had risen—Lila was her employee—he laughed. "Oh, so you're on your way to a movie with your nurse."

"Shh. Don't ruin things before they start."

Cade held back a chuckle. Though it was weird watching his dad behave like a normal middle-aged man, Cade liked seeing him happy. "All right. I'll call Mom and let her know I'm coming home."

He disconnected the call as they reached the patio. Facing Reese, he said, "Give me ten minutes to call my mom."

She leaned in and kissed him. "Sure. I'll run upstairs and put on a bathing suit."

He caught her hand and pulled her back to him for another kiss. "Or not. I'm not opposed to skinny-dipping."

She laughed and headed into the house.

Cade dropped to a chaise lounge. He hit the contact button for his mom and in a few seconds her face appeared on his screen. It was clear she had been crying.

"Cade? What's wrong?"

"I'm fine. I'm calling about you."

She batted a hand in dismissal. "Oh, I'm okay." She peered at the screen, as if trying to see over his shoulder. "Where *are* you?"

"I'm at the island with Reese—"

"Reese Farrell?"

"You know another Reese?"

"Oh, my goodness. No wonder you look so happy."

"I am happy. But don't go overboard. We just saw each other for the first time in twelve years."

"You know, all twelve of those years I felt bad because I was pretty sure our divorce battles had something to do with your breakup. It's good to see you get a second chance."

The words *second chance* sent anxiety scurrying through him. It was impressions like that—reactions like that—that could ruin everything for two people who weren't looking for a commitment.

"Mom—"

She shook her head again. "Sometimes I don't think you realize how lucky you are. You have everything. You're smart. You're handsome—"

"You're my *mother*. Of course you think that." Stopping that discussion before she blew things out of proportion, he said, "Dad just called to say you and the preacher weren't an item anymore."

Her face fell. "Your dad knows?" She took a quick breath, looked at the ceiling and said, "Stupid old goat probably told everyone from the pulpit at tonight's service."

Cade frowned. "I don't think it's wise to call a man of the cloth a stupid old goat."

"He *is* a stupid old goat. Do you know what he told me? That I wasn't marriage material, and that people were talking about us."

"Isn't being the center of attention your thing? You usually like hearing that people are talking about you."

"Not this time. Not this way! Cade, I changed completely for that man."

"Maybe you should be glad it's over? You can go back to being yourself."

"That's the point. I loved being the person I was with him. I loved that life." She paused, then shook her head. "I loved him."

He saw that in her face. Not the love. The loss of love. The genuine pain that hadn't been there when she and his dad divorced.

"I'm sorry."

"Yeah. Me too."

"Hey, maybe you should just pack up and come down to the island? We're leaving but maybe that's good. You'll have the whole place to yourself."

"Or I could bring some girlfriends and we could drown our sorrows in margaritas." She sighed. "I haven't had a drink the whole time I dated that man."

Cade blinked, realizing the level to which his mom had changed, but he also heard the sadness in her voice.

"Anyway, the island is yours. Bring your friends. Call housekeeping and tell them to stock the place full of tequila and triple sec."

She laughed. "I guess that would be better than sitting around here feeling worthless."

He remembered that feeling very well. After Reese had dumped him, he'd felt like he had no meaning in his life. Luckily, he hadn't merely found it in his studies. Wyatt and Trace and their big ideas had brought him back to life.

"Call your friends."

"Right. Okay. I love you, kiddo."

"I love you too."

The sadness in her voice stayed with him after he hung up the phone. He rose from the chaise when Reese came to the patio wearing a little blue bikini. "Thought I said remove everything."

She laughed and dived into the pool. "You were also on a video call with your mom."

"Oh, right."

He stepped out of his shorts, then unbuttoned his shirt and tossed it and his shorts toward the kitchen entryway before he dived in with her.

He swam to her, reached behind her and had her bikini top off in what he knew was record time.

She swatted his hands. "Hey! Don't I get a little sweet talk?"

"No-bake cookies."

Her face scrunched. "What?"

"No-bake cookies. They're sweet."

She laughed and shook her head. "You're so weird."

She sounded so much like her sixteen-year-old self that his heart filled with memories that dissolved into present-day emotion. He'd never felt about anyone the way he'd felt about her. "No. You're wonderful."

She eased over to him, wrapping her arms around his neck. "That's better."

He kissed her. All the emotion he felt when she'd laughed over his no-bake cookie joke filled him with a crazy joy. It was everything he could do not to tell her he loved her.

But just like his desire to ask her what was

wrong the night before when she was tossing and turning, he knew some things were off-limits. Some things would draw them too close. Some things could give her the wrong idea.

He let the kiss go on as he slid her bikini bottoms down her thighs until she could kick them off. They seemed to drift endlessly. With nowhere to go and no one trying to reach them, their world was peaceful and silent. So perfect it was as if time stood still.

Treading water, Reese walked her fingers up Cade's chest. "Getting dark. Looks like we'll be making love in the moonlight."

He caught her hand, not sure of the significance of that. "Oh, yeah?"

She met his gaze with warm green eyes. "Don't you remember us talking about that?"

As the memory materialized, he yanked her to him, pressing her against his chest. "Vaguely." They'd been kids, with very adult dreams, wishing for some very adult things. "We knew it would never happen, though... Privacy issues."

Her breathing became unsteady. "Yeah. Your parents were always home at night. But there's no one here now." She glanced around with a laugh. "*Really* no one here except you and me. How many people do you know who buy their own island just to make sure they call the shots?"

"Hey, Trace bought a vineyard in his favorite part of the world. It's at least five times the size of this island. To me, it's no different."

She eased against him to nibble his neck. "Maybe."

He kissed her. Slowly at first, then the kiss deepened, as he realized what she'd said was true. He did a lot of things to control his life, control his world. Even the way he continually monitored his feelings for her, making sure they didn't go too far.

But that was working. It kept them from saying or doing something that would ruin their time together. Only an idiot screwed with something that was working.

They made love slowly with him thinking about perfection. All the years he'd had this house he'd believed it was utopia. With her here, it was perfection. The distinction was slight, but enough that he felt it, enjoyed it.

An hour later, in the master suite, they showered off the pool water, and the scent of her bodywash filled the room. He inhaled deeply, savoring it and her chatter about going home to a ton of paperwork.

As she combed out her wet hair, he listened

and laughed with her, then suddenly all he could do was stare at her.

He was going to miss her.

Not in the sense that they'd had fun and he wished it could continue. He would go back to Manhattan knowing he'd left a piece of himself behind. His penthouse would be cold and empty. The city would be a cacophony of noise that had no meaning. Nothing would make him laugh.

Nothing would make him *feel*.

Pushing that out of his brain, he led her to bed and she fell asleep almost instantly. But he couldn't stop thoughts of how difficult it would be when he returned to Manhattan, where his life was work and more work.

He suddenly understood what had happened with Trace. Why he'd left Manhattan for Italy to purchase a vineyard in the place that called to his soul. Then he'd found the love of his life and changed everything about the way he lived.

More than that, Cade finally saw what his mom had been trying to articulate. She'd found love and lost it. And now her life was back to being cold, empty. Margaritas with friends where there had once been purpose and meaning. The warmth of companionship. The closeness of someone you wanted to be with and who wanted to be with you—

What he had with Reese—the connection, the click—wasn't something that came along every day. He wasn't engaged in life without her. He wasn't *happy* without her. He was okay. His life was good. But he wasn't really *happy*.

But with her? Everything was better. Brighter. Filled with promise.

And he was going to walk away? Be like his mom? Always on the cusp of something wonderful, but never living it.

The thought shocked him, but he realized that's what his crazy musings all week had been about. He'd been working to figure out what had been under his nose all along. He *did* want everything he and Reese had planned when they were kids. Not because he wanted a family or to become a dad, but because their pairing was unique and wonderful, and he didn't need six weeks or a year to figure that out. He'd seen it at eighteen.

And he had to act. Right now. Before she went home. Before either one of them had too much chance to think so much they ruined the truth of it.

He loved her. He had always loved her. And she loved him.

They belonged together.

She stirred beside him and he realized she was awake.

"I think you should marry me."

She laughed and nestled against him. The feeling of rightness, of permanence, suddenly filled the room, as if it had been hovering, waiting for him to see it.

He sat up, taking her with him. "Don't you feel it? We belong together. Granted, we might not want to get married tomorrow. But there's no reason we can't seal the deal today."

Reese blinked at him. She'd been jarred out of her light sleep, but she could swear he'd just said they should get married.

She blinked again.

His earnest eyes held hers. "I love you."

He said it slowly as if it surprised him, but also filled him with a sort of desperation, and her heart swelled with longing. She understood why he wanted them to make a commitment of sorts right now. The last time they'd felt this way, fate had screwed them royally. He didn't want to risk losing what they had again.

He also realized there was something else hiding in the shadows, waiting to ruin their lives again. He'd alluded to it. She'd avoided conversations. He didn't have to have insider knowledge or a keen sixth sense. She hadn't been subtle about the way she dodged his questions.

Of course he was desperate. He wanted to seal the deal before her secret ruined everything.

She had to swallow before she could say, "I love you too."

Gripping her shoulders, he pulled her to him and kissed her. Deeply, passionately, with the familiarity of someone who knew her. Someone who wanted her. Someone who loved her so much he ached with it.

He broke away, saying, "Seems to me there's a proposal on the table."

She blinked back tears and pulled away. Part of her begged her to take a chance, roll the dice, tell him the truth.

The other part didn't want to see the look of disappointment or feel the pain of rejection. She just wanted this week. Something she could hold in her heart and think about when she was lonely.

"Cade, you know I don't want to get married. We already talked about this, remember?"

He studied her for a few seconds before he said, "Do you think this is a fluke? That there isn't a reason we ended up here together?"

She pushed herself to be light, to shift his

focus, so she could get herself out of this discussion before the conversation went too far. "There *was* a reason we're here together. Your dad."

"He might have gotten us here, but we picked up the rest. We've always belonged together. Our breakup might have separated us for a while, but we couldn't be in the same house for two days without gravitating together.

"You said you wouldn't let Finn steal any more of your life than he already had. Well, this is another piece. Another thing he stole. Had that night not happened, you and I would have stayed together, married, had kids. This is what should have happened. All those dreams we talked about while swimming at the Colonial? All those plans we made? I want them. I don't want Finn to steal anything else from me."

She stiffened, easing away from him. He'd told her he loved her, but the more he explained, the more it seemed he wanted them to go back in time, back to something that couldn't be.

"This isn't about Finn. Not anymore."

"Then what's it about?"

Her gaze drifted back to his. To his unbelievably handsome face. To those earnest eyes. He might have seen a difficult side of life with his parents, but he'd never really known trouble.

To him life was simple. Find something you want, go after it.

While her life could be a study in compromise. Have dreams...realize they'll never materialize. Find something you want...lose it. Tell someone your truth...be humiliated.

Figure out what you can have—realistically—and settle for that.

That's what her life was. Settling.

He huffed a bit and fell back to his pillow. "I will wear you down."

Which was exactly what she was afraid of. She turned to look at him, naked, sprawled on his enormous bed, the symbol of his wealth. But also his intelligence and kindness and generosity.

The urge to throw herself into his arms and accept his proposal roared through her. Except she had a secret. In a way, having no one know she couldn't have children hid a big part of her. It protected her, sure. But she'd suffered alone in silence. This might be her chance to end that.

Or to end her relationship with him, when he couldn't accept her as she was. Especially after nothing more than a vacation fling.

She took a breath. She had a choice. Tell him or bail before she had to. There was no middle of the road here.

Sliding her phone off the bedside table, she got out of bed and headed into the bathroom. She flushed the toilet to keep Cade at bay but also to cover her phone call to Dennis, who told her he could be there in thirty minutes.

Thirty minutes.

She would pack and be gone in thirty minutes because she could not share the truth with him. Not yet. Maybe after a few trips here together, weeks or months of getting reacquainted, she would be able to confide in him. But not now.

Not until he was ready to hear it and she was ready to say it.

She turned toward the bathroom door. Cade stood leaning against the jamb. "Is this another one of those times you're not going to tell me what's wrong?"

"Yes." She took a breath and smiled, taking the sting out of what she had to say. "We need to spend a little more time together before we spill *all* our secrets."

He groaned. "Come on. We are older, smarter than we were when we were teenagers. You know it as well as I do. We blew our first chance. But we turned out okay and now we're back. There isn't anything you can't tell me."

Her heart lifted as the new, mature Cade surfaced. Maybe she could tell him?

She licked her lips. "Okay."

"So, spill."

She slid her T-shirt over her head to give herself a breath of time to think it through. Everything he'd said so far had been about belonging together. He'd said he loved her. And she believed that. But he had to say something that would make her feel that the love he had for her wasn't just lust mixed with happiness. That it was something that could survive hearing she couldn't have children.

"I want to."

"Then do it!"

She studied his face, working up the courage to tell him. But she remembered how Tony had worshipped the ground she walked on and after one sentence stepped back, away from her. They'd dated an entire year before they'd gotten to that point. She and Cade had spent a week together.

If what she and Tony had couldn't survive, how could the nostalgia of one week get her and Cade through this?

When she didn't answer, he ran his hand along the back of his neck. "I'm not sure what you want me to say."

That you love me for me?

That we could face anything together?

That nothing would ever break us apart again?

"I know what happened with Finn scarred you. I wouldn't for one second downplay that. But you told me that and we worked through it."

Except he'd gotten it all wrong at first. He'd sympathized instead of seeing her strength and courage. If he pitied her now, she'd melt into a ball of sorrow.

"We need time."

"We don't have time. I have this horrible sense that if I let you go now, you'll never come back."

"To this beautiful island? Of course I will!"

"Don't be flip! It's our breakup all over again. You having a secret and instead of facing it you run!"

She froze.

Dear God, he was right. Because of Tony's reaction, she'd never told another soul she couldn't have children. She'd run. Hidden.

Just as she had after being raped.

She thought back to those weeks after Finn had violated her. Thought back to how she'd desperately wanted to tell Cade, but he hadn't called and, in the end, she'd realized she'd always felt a little uncomfortable being the poor girl dating the rich kid. They'd come from two different worlds. Had two different sets of life experiences.

She hadn't kept her secret about being raped because she'd lost her nerve. She'd lost her nerve because she'd never felt secure in Cade's love.

Was that what was actually happening now? That deep down she was realizing that she couldn't tell him she couldn't have kids? Not just because she didn't want to disappoint him. But because she didn't want to face the fact that she didn't really belong with him.

Wasn't the right person for him.

Never had been.

"We are lucky to love each other the way we do. We cannot walk away from this. Not when we can have all the things we talked about twelve years ago, great jobs, a strong marriage and a family. Kids to love and cuddle and train to be great people."

He was like a happy yellow Lab. Filled with crazy enthusiasm, he saw nothing but perfection in their future. She remembered this side of him and knew that was really what had broken them up the first time. Being raped marred the perfection he saw. Perfection she always knew she didn't have. Rather than tell him, she broke up with him.

Now, she had a secret that would mar his view again.

Her voice a soft whisper, she said, "The future you think you see with me will never happen and maybe that was our problem all along. The only trouble you ever really saw was from two parents behaving badly. Any problem you had you could solve with money. But some problems are about more than throwing money at them and hoping they'll disappear. Real life can get ugly."

He blinked in surprise. "Well, that's not fair."

"Life's not fair."

He stepped closer. "This is why I knew we needed to have the big talk right now. To work some things out before you bolted. I realized yesterday that something was bothering you. If I'm honest, I'd seen it a time or two before that too. I gave you your privacy. I never asked. But I'm asking now."

She stared up at him. Saw those earnest eyes again. Took a breath. Knew it didn't matter how he reacted; they didn't belong together. "I can't have kids."

Cade only stared at her. His long pause made her so raw and so vulnerable, she trembled. But he looked gobsmacked—so shocked he couldn't speak.

He couldn't handle it.

And she couldn't handle him placating her.

She turned away, tossing toiletries into her suitcase. "I called Dennis. He said he'd be here in thirty minutes. That was ten minutes ago. I need the rest of the time to get ready to leave."

"Dennis can wait!"

"It's nighttime. He needs to get me to the airport and go home to his kids. And I want to get home. I've got work to do."

The way she talked about simple, ordinary things when something so important hovered in the air baffled him until he realized she was locking him out. She *had* locked him out.

"Don't do this."

She turned and smiled at him, though her smile was weak, her eyes were empty. "I'm just leaving as we said I would."

But he knew with the certainty of a man on death row that he would never see her again.

She rolled her suitcase to the door. Smiled again. "I'll catch you next time I'm here."

She walked down the steps and he bounded after her. "No! My God, Reese! How can you tell me something like that and just walk away?"

She pulled in a long breath. "I've known this for six years. You're just finding out now. I think you need a little time to process everything, and I need to get home. To get back to work. I stayed a day longer than I was supposed to. My staff's probably pulling out their hair without me."

He barely listened to the hollow excuse. "I know what you're doing. You're shutting me out. Just like you did twelve years ago."

She acted as if she didn't hear him. She was in the garage and had her suitcase in the back basket of a bike before he could stop her.

That was when he realized he hadn't dressed. He couldn't cycle to the helicopter pad naked. He raced upstairs and jumped into shorts and flip-flops before rushing to the garage for a bike.

Pedaling faster than she could, he nearly caught up to her. But Dennis was waiting. He grabbed her suitcase with a grin, asking about her trip.

"It was great," Reese said, as if she hadn't just had one of the most serious conversations of her life. As if everything in her life was fine when Cade knew it wasn't.

They ran to the helicopter and disappeared inside.

Cade watched her leave in the darkness, too shell-shocked to be sad…but also seeing things he'd never noticed before. She was the strongest, most stubborn person he'd ever met. If she wanted to power through this, she would. She could pretend for all the world that she was a happy businesswoman, taking care of other people.

Because that was how she hid. That was how she survived.

But it also hit him that every time she'd needed him, he hadn't been there for her. He'd tried tonight but he'd been stunned. And she was one step ahead of him. Always one step ahead of him. Maybe because he'd never been confronted by a real problem, so he didn't know how to respond, react, quickly enough to stop the damage?

Reese had said it.

He'd never had a real problem, never hit a road-block to what he wanted, and tonight he'd come face-to-face with one he had absolutely no idea how to handle. What to say. How to stop her.

He thought back to their conversation. He recognized he must have gone off track, said something that shut her down. But he didn't know what—

Or why.

He reminded himself of his dad. Good at business. Bad with relationships. Really bad with sticking his foot in his mouth.

Which might make Reese correct. If he really was as clueless as his dad, maybe they weren't right for each other?

Maybe she deserved someone better?

CHAPTER FOURTEEN

REESE HAD TO wait until Sunday morning to get a flight. She arrived in Ohio Sunday afternoon, feeling like Cinderella the day after the ball. Except she hadn't left behind a glass slipper. Cade would not be searching the kingdom of Oilville, Ohio, looking for her. He now knew they weren't meant to be together. She wasn't who he thought she was. She could not give him a child. She was willing to try a workaround. Use a surrogate. Adopt. But with hours to think it through, he hadn't so much as phoned her to suggest it.

If she caved and called him, because she loved him, because she wanted him, she would never feel understood or loved. She would always feel she had to work to keep his love, rather than rest easy in the fact that she had it.

She unpacked and called her assistant, who filled her in on everything that had happened the days she was gone. Nothing unusual. Nothing pressing.

She disconnected the call and ran her hands down her face. Eight days ago, this job was her life. Taking care of people satisfied her. Now?

Now she was confused and empty. With a wound in her heart that she didn't know how to heal. She couldn't lock this away in a box. It wasn't a bad memory. It was a true loss. A gaping hole. A longing for things to be different when she above all people knew that sometimes things couldn't *be* different. You had to play the hand you were dealt.

Her phone rang and she reached for it, looked at Martin Smith's smiling face and groaned. Not ready to deal with him, she hit Dismiss Call and picked up a stack of bills her computer spit out based on the billable hours input into her system by her employees.

Her phone rang again.

Martin again.

She hit Dismiss Call.

Her phone rang again. She saw Martin's smiling face and groaned.

The man was like a bad cold.

She clicked to answer the call. "What!"

"Hey, I just wanted to see if you enjoyed your time at the island. Stayed more than a week!" he said excitedly. "Did you have fun?"

She put her elbow on her desk and her chin on her closed fist. She considered lying. She considered yelling at him. Instead, she took a cleansing breath and said, "You shouldn't have meddled."

"Meddled?"

"Does playing matchmaker ring any bells?"

"So, what you're saying is that it didn't work."

"No. Martin. I'm saying you shouldn't have set us up."

"Why? My boy do something?"

She sighed. "No. He was… We had fun."

"Reese," Martin said softly. "I'm hearing love in your voice."

She said nothing as tears swelled in her eyes.

"It's what I want for my boy. I've always known it was a mistake for the two of you to break up. And it was my fault. Mine and Marge's. I wanted to fix it."

"Yeah, well, maybe it wasn't a mistake for us to split. I can't be what he wants. What he needs. What he deserves."

"He deserves a woman who loves him and as a guy who's never had that I'm speaking from experience."

"Goodbye, Martin."

"Reese… Wait!"

"Goodbye."

Exhausted, she climbed the stairs, shed her clothes and took a long, hot shower in her simple shower/tub combo. She hadn't grown so accustomed to the luxury of Cade's island that she couldn't come back to the plain but adequate system. She'd never had delusions of grandeur. She could live in an RV and be happy. But she missed Cade. She missed that feeling of connection. She missed his friendship and his passion.

He'd made her feel loved, supported, sexy, then just like the last time, reality took it all away. He didn't understand, *couldn't* understand that she didn't want long discussions. She wanted him to love her unconditionally. She'd wanted him to hear she couldn't have kids and love her anyway.

When he hadn't, all those feelings of inadequacy from twelve years ago had returned.

And why not? She really wasn't who he thought she was.

Instead of picking up her normal routine on Monday morning, she sent a new nurse to Martin's house. She couldn't send Lila, not after a Saturday night movie date, but she also didn't feel like facing more of Martin's inquisition.

At exactly the time the nurse should have arrived, Martin called her. When she didn't answer, he called her again. She turned off her phone.

Cup of coffee in hand, still in her pajamas, she walked into her silent office and took a seat at the desk. That's when it settled in on her that she was alone. Really alone. Not because she didn't have anybody, but because no one really knew her. As long as she kept secrets, she would always be one step removed from everyone in her life. Never be close to anyone. She'd tried telling her secret once and lost the only man since Cade who'd supposedly loved her. Cade might not have said she was worthless the way Tony had, but he'd also never told her she was okay. Perfect the way she was. The woman he wanted no matter the circumstances.

But how could he say it? She'd held back something important and when she'd told him, she was no longer the person he thought she was.

A vital twenty-eight-year-old woman who could give him a child.

Now she was a shadow of who he'd thought she was.

Hours later, when Reese was knee-deep in reviewing the billable hours report her computer had posted after spitting out bills and payroll checks, her doorbell rang.

Tired of looking at numbers, she rose, stretched and headed for the door.

The bell rang again.

"I'm coming! Keep your pants on!"

She opened the door. When she saw Cade, her heart lifted, then sank like a stone. She hated that she'd admitted her deepest, darkest secret to him. Hated that she'd shocked him to the point that he could barely respond. Hated that she wasn't the person he'd believed she was.

Hated even more that he looked fabulous. Not because he was good-looking, though he was, but because every fiber of her being yearned to see him, yearned to touch him, yearned for him to love her.

"I understand you being angry with me."

She shook her head. "Cade, seriously, I've had enough. I can't go over this one more time."

"Okay, then how about this? I love you."

Her heart ached. She loved him too. In some ways, she believed she'd been waiting for him to come back to her. But that didn't change the fact that she couldn't have kids. That she felt worthless. Empty. Less than. She knew those feelings were wrong. She knew that eventually she would have to overcome them, that maybe losing Cade was the key to figuring out how. He'd been shocked when she'd told him she couldn't give him kids. How could she expect him to say she was perfect the way she was? When she wasn't?

"Love doesn't solve everything."

"I think you're wrong."

His answer was so unexpected, she laughed.

"Look, Reese. Maybe I see this differently than you do, but I don't think I'm wrong. You're not broken. You're you. Perfect the way you are. Everything else is part of life."

She stared at him. She'd heard him say *perfect*. The simple word had stopped her heart. But it was what he'd said after that stalled her breath. "Part of life?"

"Sure. If you can't have what you want, you don't go through life longing for it. Other things pop up. That doesn't make them less than the first thing you wanted. In fact, sometimes the second thing you get is better than the first ever would have been." He sighed. "Is anything I'm saying making sense enough that you'll let me in your house? So we can take this off the porch?"

His answer wasn't flip or offhand. He'd done some deep thinking about this. Her heart lifted a little more.

She stepped back, allowing him entry. It was a risk to let him in, but her aching heart couldn't turn him away. Not when there was a chance that he really did understand.

He walked in but waited until the door had been closed before he said, "I realized that I'd proposed all wrong on Saturday night. My mom had said something about me not appreciating that I have everything and that night I saw that we belonged together. I proposed before I gave you a chance to get adjusted to us. But I know this is what I want. What I've always wanted. I lost you once because I got the whole situation wrong. I won't lose you again for the same reason."

Oh, he was such a dreamer.

"It's not the same. You might have misinterpreted the first time because I never told you about Finn. But not being able to have kids is the reality of my life."

"No. It's the reality of your body. But it's not the reality of your life. Everything about you suits me. You make me laugh. You talked me through a difficult time. You don't like to fish but you love being on the boat. And there are going to be things you like that I don't... But all that does is give us a chance to be ourselves so that when we do have time together, we'll love it all the more."

Her eyes began to fill. She tried blinking away the tears, but he held her gaze. His heart in his eyes.

"We fit. We always fit. And, honestly, though

eighteen-year-old me was so preoccupied with school that he didn't see you were drowning, I'm not that kid anymore. I've grown up. I'd do anything for you. Fight anyone for you. But most of all I just want the chance to love you."

Her chin wobbled as sobs tried to overtake her. She said nothing. Only stared at him. Longing for everything they could have together tightened her chest. She wanted to jump into his arms and weep... But the memory of being let down held her back.

"Hey. If my dad can change, I sure as hell can change."

She laughed through her tears.

"Come here."

He held out his arms and she stepped into them. Warmth suffused her as the longing to believe him pressed so hard her chest hurt.

"Not being able to have children doesn't make you less than. It simply means we look at other options. You are whole and perfect as you are."

The logjam of pain and tears building in her chest and eyes burst and she began to cry in earnest.

"You aren't just my rock. You hold my heart. And you are my soul. Part of me will never forgive myself for letting you down twelve years ago, but I think that just means I won't screw up this time."

That made her laugh and she leaned back to peer up at him. "The worst thing anyone can ever do is promise perfection. It's unattainable."

He loosened his hold on her so he could capture her gaze. "Okay. How about this. I promise to love you. Just as you are. Forever."

"That's a good promise."

"Right now, you could give me the reciprocal promise. I'm on as shaky ground as you are. You are everything I've ever wanted—"

She bounced to her tiptoes and pressed her lips to his. She tried to keep it simple but it shifted to intense within seconds. Tongues twining, their past, present and future merged.

"You are the most kind, loving person in the world. I'm so happy with you. Could we just enjoy that for a while?"

"Yes."

He kissed her again, then took a step back. "And I just want to clarify… This isn't a second chance. This is a new beginning. But I found this at the jeweler last night—"

He pulled a locket from his pocket. A heart similar to the one he'd given her when they were teenagers.

"Oh, my God."

"It's not the one I gave you originally. I didn't keep it. Bad feelings attached to it and all that." He laughed and looped the new locket around her neck. "I wish I had the first one. Because it's a touchstone. A reminder of what we knew in our guts all those years ago. That we belong together."

She laughed through her tears. "Agreed. This locket is enough to seal our relationship."

He shook his head. "Does that mean you don't want this?" He pulled out a box with a diamond engagement ring.

Her gaze leaped to his. "I thought we were taking this slowly?"

He shrugged. "We are. Sort of. But I want the commitment. I never want to let you go. But I also never want any doubt between us about who we are and that we belong together."

She threw her arms around him again. "I do love you and we do belong together. I want the commitment too."

He said, "Thank God," then he kissed her and everything in both of their worlds righted.

EPILOGUE

THE HOSPITAL'S LABOR and delivery room was nothing like Reese expected. She knew Cade had pulled strings to get a private room, but she didn't realize they'd be spending the entire adventure in one place. No operating room. No delivery room. Just a homey little space that looked like someone's bedroom.

Meredith Oliver groaned and rubbed her hands across her belly. "Here comes another contraction."

Reese lifted her shoulders and caught her gaze. "Breathe. Remember? Like this."

Meredith mimicked the quick, shallow breaths Reese demonstrated. She and Cade had chosen her to be the surrogate for their baby because she was older, closer to thirty-five than twenty-five, and settled. She and her husband had two children they adored. Grateful and happy, they wanted to give back. Going through the process with her had been like having a smart tour guide.

The contraction stopped and Meredith took a long cleansing breath before she squeezed Reese's hand. "I told you this was a piece of cake."

Cade's phone rang and he walked away as Reese squeezed Meredith's hand in return. She already knew how grateful they were that she'd agreed to be surrogate for their little boy. She and her family had become such a part of Reese's and Cade's lives that Reese knew their friendship would last forever.

Standing close to the door, Cade said, "Are you sure?"

Reese glanced over.

Meredith shook her head. "I hope he's not making some kind of big deal with Wyatt and Trace."

"He promised he wouldn't." She smiled at Meredith. "And he never breaks his promises."

"We're going to have to get him to teach Jim that," she said, referring to her husband.

Cade strolled over. "Teach Jim what?"

Reese slid her arm around his waist, including him in their birthing group. "How to keep all his promises."

"You have really got to stop telling people about that. You're ruining all my street cred in Man World."

Meredith laughed as Cade pulled Reese away from the bed. "We need to talk."

"We do?"

"Yes. That call was from an adoption agency. A woman has chosen us to be her baby's parents."

"I thought we took ourselves off the lists."

"Looks like we missed one."

Reese blinked and finally saw the gob-smacked look on Cade's face.

She laughed. "What? Are you panicking?"

"No. Yes..." He ran his hand along the back of his neck. "She's due in two weeks. We'll have two babies at the same time."

"We'll raise them like twins."

He gaped at her. "You're okay with this?"

"We were planning on having a few children. Having two only a few weeks apart will be fun." She nudged him. "It's not like we can't afford help."

He let that settle in for a few seconds, then he laughed and pulled out his phone and redialed the adoption agency number. "When do you need us in New York?" He paused, slipped his hand around Reese's waist and winked at her. "We'll be there."

When he clicked off the call, he said, "I hope you're ready for this."

"I hope *we're* ready for this."

He laughed and they edged back to the bed,

where Meredith was experiencing another contraction. The doctor came in, put on rubber gloves and examined Meredith.

"Okay. Looks like we're ready."

Reese looked at Cade.

Cade looked at Reese. "See? Even he knows we're ready."

* * * * *

*If you missed the previous story in the
A Billion-Dollar Family trilogy,
then check out*

Tuscan Summer with the Billionaire

*And if you enjoyed this story, check out
these other great reads from
Susan Meier*

Stolen Kiss with Her Billionaire Boss
Hired by the Unexpected Billionaire
The Bodyguard and the Heiress

All available now!